DANGEROUS ATTRACTION

CLUB PRIVÉ 8

M. S. PARKER

BELMONTE PUBLISHING, LLC

Copyright © 2016 Belmonte Publishing LLC

Published by Belmonte Publishing LLC

READING ORDER

Thank you so much for reading the Club Privé series. If you'd like to read the complete series, I recommend reading them in this order:

1. Intrigued
2. Exposed
3. Chasing Perfection
4. Craving Perfection
5. Finding Perfection
6. French Connection
7. Unlawful Attraction
8. Dangerous Attraction
9. A Legal Affair
10. A Legal Romance
11. Collide
12. Enticed

ONE

ARIK

Good-bye, Arik.

Staring at her back, my blood pulsing through my veins, I told myself to take a few minutes to think it through.

Hell no.

It only took a few strides to catch up with her. She'd settled back over at the railing, staring down over the dance floor with a look of patent boredom on her face. She was clearly trying hard to pretend she didn't care.

Or maybe that was just my wishful thinking.

When I touched her shoulder, she gave a long-suffering sigh before slanting a look up at me. "What?"

I bristled at her tone. "You sound like you're having a pleasant day."

"Not that it's any of your business." The pointed expression on her face might've scared a lesser man off.

Fortunately, I wasn't a lesser man.

"I think it's time the two of us had a little chat." I put my mostly-empty drink down on the nearby railing, but when I tried to touch her cheek, she jerked a hand up, catching my wrist with a speed that I had to admit was fairly impressive.

"Hands off," she said bitingly.

"Okay." Lowering my hand to the railing on the other side of her, I leaned in and studied her face. "Is that a permanent thing, or are you just having a bitchy day?"

I doubled over as she drove an elbow into my stomach, then ducked under my arm and moved away. I was more caught off guard than in pain though, and my stunned disbelief only lasted a few seconds.

Grabbing her arm, I caught her and jerked her back before she could take off. "Okay, sweetheart. How about you explain just what the ever-loving fuck that was about?"

She tried to twist out of my grasp, but all it did was put her pelvis in close proximity to mine, reminding both of us of just what happened when the two of us were together. Her breath caught and I slid a hand up her back, tangling my fingers in her short hair.

"Keep moving like that, Dena. I'm enjoying it. It's been a little too long since I've been able to bury my dick inside you."

A second later, I tasted blood as she slammed the heel of her hand against my chin. I bit my tongue and pain flared.

"Alright, that's it." Spinning her around, I caught her wrists and twisted them behind her back. I lowered my mouth to her ear, desire and anger pulsing inside me. "What's with the guerrilla tactics, Dena?"

"Let me go," she said, a warning note in her voice.

I'd never been one to hold a woman against her will, but I knew if I didn't push her, I'd lose her. Lowering my head, I whispered against her ear, "Make me."

She stiffened instead. When it became clear she wouldn't do anything, I swore and pulled back, giving her a few inches of space. She took that space and tried to walk away again.

"I don't think so." I stepped around her, cutting her off as I planted myself in her path. I glared down at her. "Just where in the hell do you think you're going?"

Her lips twisted into an unpleasant scowl. "I'm going anywhere that isn't here."

"Fine. I'll go with you. We need to talk."

"No." She shook her head. "We don't."

Closing the small distance between us, I stared down at her, but if I thought my height would be intimidating, I was underestimating her. She just tipped her head back and crossed her arms.

"Look, Mr. Porter—"

"Arik."

She arched her brows. "*Arik*? I'm sorry. I was under the impression you wanted me to address you as *Mr. Porter*, given our professional relationship."

It was only then I saw the depth of anger in her eyes.

Oh shit. I'd seriously fucked things up with her.

None of that should've mattered. We weren't in a relationship. We fucked. That was it. No commitments, no explanations.

Then why did I feel like I'd done something wrong?

"Dena, we need to talk," I said, softening my voice. "Especially about that."

"No." She reached up and patted my cheek. "We don't. See, *that* is really all there is. You have a good night."

She turned away. Again. I was really getting sick of her doing that. I caught her arm, but this time, when I whirled her back to face me, she came back swinging.

My head flew back from the impact of her fist against the side of my face, but I didn't let go.

"Did that make you feel any better?" I demanded as I gingerly touched my jaw. It was pounding and from the corner of my eye, I could see her flexing her fingers. If my face was any indication of how hard she'd hit me, her hand had to be hurting.

"Why, yes, actually." She gave me a slow smile that didn't reach her eyes. "I feel better than I have in several days. Thank you for asking." She jerked on her arm. "Now let me go."

I tightened my grip, aware that if I squeezed any harder, I'd bruise her. And not in a good way. "Not until you calm down and agree to talk to me."

"Not on your *life*," she snapped.

"Dammit, Dena!"

"Is there a problem here?"

Both of us looked up.

As Gavin emerged from the crowd that had gathered around us, I uncurled my fingers from her arm and let my hand drop to my side. He gave me a pointed glare before looking over at Dena.

She made a face at him. "No problem, Gavin."

"And that's why you hit one of my guests in the face?" he asked, sounding almost amused.

She curled her lip. "He asked for it."

"Did he now?"

Carrie was with us now and she looked between us before moving to Dena's side. She caught Dena's hand and lifted it. "Oh, honey."

Gavin's presence was enough to disperse the crowd, but I barely saw them go. I was looking at Dena's hand, my gut twisted in a bunch of slippery knots. Her knuckles were already swelling. Carrie waved at somebody, gripping Dena's hand tightly when she tried to pull away.

"The two of you want to tell me what's going on?" Gavin asked.

"Difference of opinion," Dena said.

"Failure to communicate."

We both spoke at the same time. Gavin's mouth flattened into a line. Aggravated, he shoved his hands into his pockets and watched Carrie press an ice pack to Dena's hand. Then his eyes slid to me.

Something told me that he wanted to make my face look like Dena's hand.

"You two are going to work this out," he finally said. "Otherwise, I'll have to revoke your guest pass, Porter. Permanently. And Dena, you'll be suspended for the next two months."

I stared at him, but Dena flinched as if he'd slapped her.

Carrie made a low sound of protest, but Gavin didn't even look at her. He was angrier than I realized.

"I was pushing too hard," I said. "I should have waited until she was calmer before I tried to talk to her. I'll leave. There's no reason to suspend her."

"There is. She violated the rules and she knows it." Gavin shrugged and held out his hand to Carrie. She hesitated, looking at him with narrowed eyes, but after a moment, she placed her hand in his. He looked back at us. "Take one of the private rooms and work whatever this is out."

As they both walked away, I turned my gaze to Dena.

She wasn't looking at me. In fact, she was trying very hard not to look at me.

After a few more seconds, I held out my hand. "Shall we?"

Dena lowered her gaze to my hand and scowled. She edged around, presenting me with a view of her narrow back as she started toward one of the private rooms. Falling into step behind her, I bit back a curse and wondered how she managed to do this to me.

I couldn't think around her.

Not at all.

She didn't look at me until she stopped in front of a door, and only then it was a glance. Still, it was enough for me to see the faint flush on her cheeks. I couldn't place the tension in her body right away, but once we stepped inside, I caught on easily enough.

The room was familiar.

In fact, it was the room I'd brought her to the first night we'd been here.

The lights were low. The bed was close by and I could instantly imagine backing her up against it, stripping her naked, tugging the slim-fitting jeans she wore down to her ankles, kissing the hollow at the base of her neck as I slid my hand inside her panties and found her wet.

I'd make her come for me before we did anything else, even before we talked. She was pissed off, angry and brittle. Hard. I didn't want her hard. I wanted her soft and wet and welcoming in my hands.

I'd make her come, then she'd cuddle up and sigh against me. I could hold her and then we could talk. Work this whole thing out.

But then she closed the door and dropped the key into a glass bowl on the low lying table near the couch. Instead of going to the bed, she settled down in an elegant sprawl on the couch and crossed one slim leg over the other.

"Well." Her lips were pursed in a mockery of a smile. "We were sent to our room, Mr. Porter. How long do you think we have to pretend to talk before we can go our separate ways?"

TWO

DENA

A muscle pulsed in his temple.

Or maybe it was a vein.

Either way, it was a clear sign he was pissed.

His jaw clenched tight and his eyes burned as he stalked toward me. Part of me wanted to draw back, but then he stilled a few feet away and I relaxed a little. I still wasn't entirely sure I should have come into this room with him. Actually, I was almost *positive* I shouldn't have come into this room with him.

But we were going to bump into each other. And he was right that we needed to talk. If not about whatever this was between us, then at least about...

"What were you doing at my client's house?" Arik demanded, the question coming out like an accusation.

I didn't remember moving. One minute I was on the couch, and the next, I was in his face, jabbing a finger into his chest. "What was *I* doing? I was doing my job. There. I answered your question." I raked him up and down, putting as much scorn into my look as I could. "Now you answer one of mine. Just how much of a coincidence was it that you showed up here right around the time I got hired at the DA's office."

Arik dipped his head, his mouth less than an inch away from mine. "I don't think I care for the accusation I'm hearing coming from you."

"Just doing the same thing you are, jackass," I snapped. "Doesn't feel very good, does it?"

I started to move away, wanting to get as far from him as possible.

Except I didn't get far.

Strong arms came around me and I bit back a gasp as he hauled me back against him. This time, I didn't dare struggle. I didn't even move. I'd felt his reaction to me out there. More, I'd been painfully aware of mine. If I pushed him too far now, we'd be all over each other in a blink and that wasn't what I wanted.

Liar.

It was a manic, delighted little voice that came from deep inside me. I wanted to throttle that voice, lock it in a trunk and throw in the Hudson, then toss the key into the sewers.

I hated it, but I couldn't actually deny it.

"What's the matter?" Arik whispered, his voice a husky purr in my ear. "Where's all that passionate fight now, Dena?"

"Let me go, Mr. Porter."

I fell back on formality, focused on the wall in front of me, hoping that maybe, just maybe, if I kept my wits intact, I could get out of this with my dignity not totally shredded. I never should have looked twice at him. I never should have looked *once* at him.

He could ruin my career.

It was already teetering thanks to Bethany. And this wouldn't be a claim I could deny.

A smooth, warm hand slid up my bare arm, higher, across my collarbone and then he placed his palm against my throat, curled his fingers. It was a terribly vulnerable position to be in, his hand around my neck. I could feel my pulse fluttering against his hand. Then he lowered his mouth and skimmed it along the curve where neck met shoulder and it took everything I had in me not to respond, not to tremble.

"Dena..." His voice was like honey. Like silk.

Fuck that.

It was pure sex.

"Let me go." I tried to demand it.

"Why?" he asked, his tone so terribly reasonable. "It seems to me you were happy here just a few days ago."

"That was before I found out you were defending a woman my office is trying for murder."

"Hmmm." His lips slid down my neck, then up.

That really shouldn't feel so good. I hated that it did.

"That is something to consider," he admitted. "But I didn't know you were an ADA, Dena. I didn't even know you were a lawyer."

His teeth caught my ear and I shuddered. For that long moment, I was so caught up in what he was doing to my body that I barely noticed his words. Heat exploded through me as he tugged on my hip, and I had to fight a whimper as he moved forward, bringing my butt in full contact with his cock.

We were both clothed. That was the only reason he wasn't already inside me, and we both knew it. I wanted him inside me so badly that it nearly hurt. I wanted to feel his cock stretching me, invading me, bringing me to another earth-shattering climax. I wanted the release that only submission to him would bring.

When he slid a hand up my belly, my breath exploded out of me in a rush.

"Did you know?"

I had no idea what he was talking about. All I knew was the feel of his touch.

His fingers popped the button on my jeans as a part of my brain screamed at me to listen.

I caught his wrist, stopping him. I was pretty sure there was a reason he didn't need to be undressing me, and I'd figure it out in a minute.

"Know what?" I managed to ask, panting in an effort to restore the flow of oxygen to my brain.

"Did you know I was a defense attorney?" His voice sounded far too serious and stable considering the fact that his fingers were tracing a path up and down the inseam of my jeans.

How could he talk about anything even remotely logical?

But then my brain locked in on just *what* he was talking about and surprisingly, my brain cleared.

I pulled away from him and took a few shaky steps. Turning toward him, I swallowed. My hands shook as I smoothed back my hair. Face burning and heart pounding, I looked around at anywhere but his face.

"If I'd known you were an attorney of *any* kind, I never would have come into one of these rooms with you, much less gotten naked with you." Pulling up the threads of my control, I managed a faint smirk. "Apparently, I need to start some sort of background check next time I get naked with a man."

Arik didn't even crack a smile.

I didn't really think it was funny either.

He came closer and reached up, shoving a hand into my hair and tangling it, tugging back until my head was cranked to a near painful angle. "My temper is already at a snapping point. Want to see me go over? Talk about getting naked with another man, Dena."

I shoved at him, disregarding the hand he had fisted in my hair.

He let go, but my scalp felt raw. "We don't have any sort of *understanding*, Mr. Porter," I said scathingly.

"We can change that."

The words caught me off guard. So much so that when he turned me around and brought me back against him, my back tucked to his chest, I didn't even think to move. It felt so good. His chest was warm and solid, heating me through and through.

"I have a hold on you now," he murmured against my ear. "I like this hold. You like it."

I did. But I shouldn't.

"You need to let me go," I said, my voice rough.

"Why?"

Why...

His question bounced around in my brain. There was a reason. I knew there was.

Finally, after far too long, I remembered.

I swallowed to loosen my tight throat before I spoke, "Because we can't be doing this. We're both working the same case – on opposite sides." My breath hitched as he rubbed his thumb across my belly through the material of my shirt.

The garment might as well have not even been there with the heat coursing through me. Struggling to think about anything that didn't involve him touching me, his hands on me, his body, I managed to drag my mind back to the present.

"We can't be doing this because it's unprofessional. I'm an ADA assigned to the prosecutor in the case. You're the defendant's lawyer. It's called conflict of interest. Surely they taught you about that in law school."

When he didn't let go, my frustration at the situation, at myself, spilled over, and it came out in a waspish bite. "Come on, unless you got your law degree from a crackerjack box or you bought it online, you know this is a problem."

"I assure you, my law degree didn't come from a box or online." He chuckled, not sounding at all offended by my words.

"You've got nasty bite to you, don't you? Keep it up, and I'll be tempted to do something about it."

His palm flexed, pulling me more firmly against him, but he spoke at the same time, distracting me from the hard, heavy pressure of his cock against the small of my back.

"What are you doing on the case, Dena? I know Bethany. She's a shark. If she smells blood in the water, she goes after it. She doesn't share." His teeth caught my ear, tugged.

I felt my knees weaken. I had to get away from him before I did something really, really stupid. Like beg him to take me.

Twisting out of his arms, I put some distance between us before looking at him. "Bethany's my boss, and she's the ADA of record on the case." My mind struggled to remember all of the legal arguments as to why we shouldn't do this. "That's enough. Besides, I was at your client's apartment. Seems like I'm plenty involved."

He didn't seem bothered at all by what I said. "Yes, you were there, but it was the weekend. Bethany thinks too much of herself to work on the weekends if she can dump it off on some-body else."

A hundred possible replies popped into my mind. Part of me wanted to tell him the truth, that I'd been moved off the case so that there was nothing keeping us apart. But I knew that this was a bad idea all the way around. I'd eventually have to face off against him.

Unless I got fired first.

Arik's eyes narrowed. "What, specifically, are your duties on this case?"

Dammit.

"Bethany wasn't pleased with some bullshit I called her on. I've been pulled from the case," I finally said, biting each word off. "I'm mostly working on research and filings with the paralegals."

"You called her on her bullshit?" He looked impressed. "What was it?"

I could tell by looking at him that he wouldn't let it go, even if he should. "You know damn well I can't tell you that." I shook my head. "See, this is why you and me and this..." Abruptly, I laughed. "There *is* no you and me. Who am I kidding?"

I was so done with this shit. I got up and started for the door.

I closed my hand around the doorknob, but his arm came over my shoulder and kept me from opening the door.

"No you and me?" His voice was low. "Are you sure about that?"

I shivered as he pressed his lips against the side of my neck.

"You don't really think you can ignore what we have between us, do you?" There was a pause, and then he added, "Do you even want to?"

I didn't bother to answer his question. Easing out from between him and the door, I turned to look at him. "I don't see why not. You asked for my number and then ignored me. I'm not one of those Subs who takes whatever a Dom dishes out. I don't sit by the phone waiting for anyone, Arik." My mouth curved into a brittle smile. "Now you tell me, how many of those nights did you spend alone? Any of them?"

"I never thought you were that kind of woman."

"That's not an answer." My chest tightened. I knew what I'd done. Or, at least, tried to do. I had no reason to doubt he hadn't done the same, no matter how much I wanted to think he hadn't.

"You want to hear that I fucked someone? Is that it?" His mouth twisted. "Fine. I did. But all I could think about was you. It was nothing more than a mindless fuck. No more than jerking off would've been."

It was a hell of a lot different than jerking off.

"Don't worry about it." I shrugged, trying not to let him see how much the thought of him with another woman hurt.

"You're not the first man who offered a line of shit to get in a woman's pants. We both had fun, so no harm, no foul, right?"

His eyes darkened and I knew he was angry at how flippant I sounded.

Too bad. Hurt shifted into anger.

Rising up onto my toes, I put my hand on his chest and pressed my lips to his ear. "Besides, it's not like I've spent every night alone pining for you."

It wasn't even a lie. Stretching the truth, maybe. But not a lie.

In a blink, I found myself pinned to the wall, his mouth a breath from mine. "I'm not the sort of man you can toy with."

My breath hissed out of me in a shocked rush as he licked my lower lip, then sucked it into his mouth. When he let go, I had to fight not to whimper.

"Do you really want to keep pushing me?" he asked, sliding a hand down my belly, his fingers pointing down so that I could feel the tips brushing over my crotch. He curled them in, and I gasped as he pressed them against me, forcing the seam of my jeans to rub into my sensitive flesh.

Swallowing, I stared at him.

He did it again, and then licked my lip, sucked it into his mouth. This time, before he let me go, he sank his teeth into the fleshy bit. He released it a little slower even as he increased the pressure of his fingers between my thighs. I couldn't swallow the moan, and my hands curled into fists as I tried not to move my hips against him.

"Tell me you met up with some guy. That you found some Sub here and let your inner Dom out. Did it help any? You sure don't feel like anybody has let you burn the edge off."

He popped the button on my jeans and dipped his hand inside. When he slid his fingers past the waistband of my panties, I closed my eyes, my head falling back as I sucked in air.

"You're so tight." His voice was rough. "I think you'd come if I just...did..."

He twisted his fingers and I felt my body tightening, ready, eager. But before I could reach it, he stopped.

"See how close you are? Tell me about the guy you were with, Dena. Did you let him get you naked? Did you suck his cock? Did he go down on you?"

I opened my eyes to mere slits and glared at him.

"You're an asshole," I said.

"That's not an answer." He pushed one knee between my thighs and shoved upward. "Unless it is. Is that it?" Jealousy laced his words. "Did you take his cock there, Dena? Up that snug, sweet ass? Did you make your Sub fuck your ass?"

I leaned in, quick as a snake, and nipped his lower lip. He responded by fisting his hand in my hair and yanking my head back. We glared at each other for a long, tense moment, and then, slowly, he lowered me back to the floor.

"I didn't pick up a Sub." I ran my tongue along my swollen bottom lip. "I found a Dom...and I brought him into one of the rooms here."

Arik growled.

"No one Dominates you but me." His voice was fierce.

I dug my nails into the back of his neck. "I don't do one-way claims, Arik."

His eyes held mine for several seconds.

And then his mouth slammed down on mine.

The next few minutes were a struggle between us. He controlled the kiss, but I didn't want to yield. I was too angry. Angry for wanting him, for not being able to have him. Angry at him for fucking another woman and at myself for caring.

He fought to free me from my clothes and after a moment, I began to tear at his shirt, then his jeans. I wasn't even sure how we managed to get our clothes off, only that they seemed to be there one moment and gone the next.

When he stopped kissing me, I swore at him. He chuckled and flipped me over, pulling me onto my hands and knees. I barely had a moment to adjust to the new position when he was there, pushing inside me with one near-brutal thrust.

He was big and hard, and I felt every ridge, every groove. I'd be feeling him inside me for days.

Suddenly, he stiffened. "Shit, Dena...I'm not...I didn't..."

He didn't have to finish the sentence. I reached back as he started to pull out, my fingers wrapping around his wrist. I looked over my shoulder at him.

"I'm on the pill. I'm clean. Are you?"

He groaned, a shudder running through him. "Yes."

I shivered at the want in his voice. Something inside felt a little broken, a little battered. Still watching his face, I opened my mouth, uncertain what I was going to say until the words came out.

"Either we have something going or we don't. If you don't want to see me for anything but this..." I gasped as he rolled his hips. "Then enjoy it. This is the last time."

"Dena," he rasped out my name as he withdrew and then slammed forward again.

Over and over, he drove into me, his fingers digging into my hips. Every inch of me was on fire, pleasure and pain coming together until I knew I wouldn't survive the explosion. There was no finesse in this, no S&M games. It was sheer domination and submission in its purest form. One person handing over control to the other with the sort of trust that rarely existed between two people.

When I came, I managed to stay upright only through sheer will and the grip of Arik's hands on my hips. Then he followed, curling his body over mine, lips pressed to my shoulder. He stayed there for a minute, not putting his full weight on me, but enough that I felt...safe. Protected.

I tried to get to my feet as he straightened, but my legs were still quivering too much to hold me. A few seconds later, I no longer needed to worry about it because he picked me up and carried me over to the bed.

Closing my eyes, I waited to hear the door close. But it didn't. Instead, I felt the dip of the bed, and then the warmth of him as he wrapped his arm around me, tucking me against his chest as he pulled a blanket over us. I tried not to think about how perfectly my body fit with his.

"What's your phone number?" he asked, his voice drowsy. "I was careless last time and forgot the paper."

"Maybe it just wasn't that important to you," I countered. "Since you were so *careless*."

"Tell me."

His tone didn't leave much room for argument, and I didn't really have the strength to push back anymore.

I told him and he recited it back.

But I didn't ask him for his number.

Not yet. I wasn't sure if I was ready.

THREE
ARIK

I'd lost track of time.

I knew it was late, and I knew both of us had slept off and on. And I knew Dena was still asleep now.

I also knew that if I was smart, I'd wake her up, because we both had a job to do in the morning and even if she was friends with the owner, I doubted they'd want us spending the whole night here. Besides, it wasn't like we could wear club clothes to work.

My stomach tightened at the thought of seeing Dena in a court room, arguing a case, while wearing those tight jeans and that shirt. I doubted a single straight man in the room would hear a word she said.

All I could care about, though, was that Dena felt amazing in my arms and I was more at peace now than I had been in a very long time. Since moving here for sure. I wasn't certain I'd ever felt this way even back in Chicago.

She made a grumbling sound under her breath, an odd noise that made me smile. I thought about maybe rolling her onto her back, spreading her thighs and licking a path down her belly to her pussy. I'd bring her close to the edge, and then bury myself inside to trigger her orgasm.

Dena closed her hand around my half-hard cock.

My breath hissed out from between my teeth as I arched up into her touch. She fisted me tight, dragging her hand up, then down. As I watched, she sat up and stared down at me, eyes heavy-lidded, hair mussed. Her bottom lip was slightly swollen and I wanted to bite it again.

"I was..." I paused, trying to gather my thoughts as she twisted her wrist just near the head and tightened her grip to just this side of painful. "Hmmmm...do that again."

She did and whatever I'd been thinking scattered. It took me a moment to regain it.

"I was thinking about waking you up."

"You missed your chance." Her voice was lower than normal, full of something deep and sexual, of something that was purely *her*.

I started to sit, but she pushed me down with a hand on my chest and threw her leg over my hips. I caught her waist, but didn't move her. I watched as she straddled me, waited to see what she was going to do next.

"I'm not in the mood for *master may I*," she said, staring at me, a defiant look in her pale eyes.

She slid against me, her cunt slick and hot.

"I..." I supported her weight as she lifted up. "I have no problem with that."

A moment later, she sank down on me, and I groaned. She was so tight, her body so small that I had to wonder how I managed to fit inside her. Then she began to move, leaning forward to give herself the leverage she wanted.

The view was mesmerizing.

There's nothing like having a woman straddle you, the way her breasts lift and move, feeling her pussy gripping your cock.

DANGEROUS ATTRACTION   21

And a woman like Dena...with her delicate features and pale skin, she looked like some sort of ethereal creature.

A faint half-smile curled her lips as she rode me, her breath catching when I arched up into her. Her fingers flexed on my chest, nails biting into my skin, sending the sweetest pricks of pain through me. She was going to leave a mark on me.

As if she hadn't already.

She panted my name and my eyes met hers. Our rhythm sped up and, all too soon, we took each other straight over the edge, ending the best damn ride of my life.

As she collapsed against my chest, I curled my arms around her and wondered if maybe I hadn't found the most perfect woman in the world.

WE STOOD on the curb outside the club, the chilly October air waking me up more than anything else had. I'd already flagged her down a cab and it sat idling at the curb. A part of me didn't want to let her go.

As she climbed inside, I leaned down after her. She gave me a sober look and I whispered her number into her ear.

Instead of the smile I'd been hoping for, I got a blank face that told me she was already pulling away.

"I'll be impressed if you actually use it," she said.

If. She said *if* rather than *when.* I couldn't be offended, though, not after the way I'd acted. But, still, there was something I wanted to know.

"You didn't ask for mine."

That blank look didn't change. "I'm not going to. Not until I know you're not being an ass again."

She shrugged and looked away.

I kissed her cheek and then pulled back, resisting the urge to take her mouth...or climb in the back with her and go back to my place where I could take more than her mouth.

After they'd pulled off into the night, I turned and started to walk. It wasn't that far to my apartment, and I needed to think.

I never should have left her number behind to begin with, and I sure as hell wasn't going to neglect calling her this time. I ran through the number again just to make sure I still had it. I'd never been with a woman who made me feel what Dena did. I couldn't even describe it, but it was...something.

Something different.

Something amazing.

Something...real.

It was time, I decided. Time to stop chasing one woman after another, time to stop bouncing around, hoping I could find more than one Sub I clicked with. Time for something more than just sex.

Although, it was funny. If I'd been looking for a woman, I never would have chosen her. I wouldn't have thought I'd be happy with a switch, somebody who had their own dominant streak, who made me work for every inch. But that was one of the things I found myself drawn to, something I wanted in a partner. A person who automatically did everything I said to do without a word had once been appealing, but I now realized that desire had stopped when I'd stopped caring only about sex and started looking for something outside the bedroom.

I wanted Dena.

FOUR
DENA

Face down in the pillows, I tried to ignore the world a little longer.

It was raining, which wasn't strange for New York in October. I could hear the persistent drops pelting my window, and the dim light that had managed to filter in through the edges of the blinds was that thin watery gray that only came with an autumn rain.

It would've been the perfect day for sleeping in, then laying around and doing nothing but reading a book, maybe watching some TV before ordering in Chinese. It was too bad I hadn't been born independently wealthy. Then I could call Bethany and tell her to kiss my ass.

I could find a hundred other ways to help people.

But I didn't have that option.

When my phone chirped, signaling a text, I flopped over onto my back and stared up at the ceiling.

It wasn't quite six which made it an awful time for anybody to be texting. It could be one of the girls, though. And if it was Krissy, that meant something was wrong.

Or she hadn't gone to bed yet and was drunk-dialing me. If

that was the case, I was going to kick her ass the next time I saw her.

If it was someone else...

Sighing, I picked up my phone.

I didn't recognize the number and the first few words creeped me the hell out. I bolted upright, pulling my blankets more tightly around me.

Then I processed the name.

Arik.

He'd signed the dirty little text.

Are you naked? If not, you should be, because I've been thinking about you naked all night. —Arik

My breath hitched a little. Shifting under the blankets, I considered the camisole and brief boy shorts I'd pulled on after my shower a few hours ago. Stretching a little, I took my time in composing a reply.

I only sleep naked if somebody is around to help me stay warm.

The clock kicked over to six, and right on time, my alarm went off. I turned it off as Arik's reply came up.

I was thinking that maybe you and I could hook up soon, maybe take some time and go away somewhere. I've got a cabin right on the edge of Lake Michigan. We could take a week up there, and I can keep you warm all night. Interested?

There was a funny, painful little twist in the vicinity of my heart. I couldn't believe how much I wanted to immediately accept the offer. The thought of an entire week with only the two of us was enough to make me even wetter than I already was.

Still, I wasn't so certain what he proposed was smart. Actually, I was pretty damn certain that it was *stupid*. It didn't make me want it any less, didn't make me want *him* any less.

I needed to stop. He was a defense attorney and I worked for the prosecution. Maybe he didn't seem too concerned about it, but I had to be. I was still trying to build my career, and the ugly truth of it was that women always came out of anything looking worse than a guy did. Especially in a career like law. And especially for a prosecutor.

Refusing to let myself even consider what he was suggesting, I tapped out a brief answer.

It wouldn't be smart, Arik. You know that. None of this is smart.

I swung my legs over the side of the bed and waited for him to answer.

He did, and surprisingly, his answer was laid back.

I find myself not caring about smart when it comes to you. We don't have to do it now. After this case is over, we can talk about it then.

Rolling my eyes, I blew out a breath. He made it seem like this case would end in the next few weeks, the next month or so. And that we would still want this then.

It's a murder trial, Arik. It could take months, longer.

A moment later, my phone rang, and I wasn't all that surprised to see it was Arik calling.

"It won't take months," he said matter-of-factly, not even bothering with a greeting. "It would be nice if you had a boss who cared about the truth, but all she cares about is winning. You strike me as a woman who does care, though. My client is innocent, Dena. I'm going to find a way to prove it, and if Bethany doesn't listen, I'll go over her head."

Which is exactly what I planned on doing if she tried to screw with things in the police report.

"I know Bethany's not going to listen to me or to you, but if you know that Leayna's innocent, I know you won't stop trying. Maybe if you find something..."

My gut twisted. Pressing my hand to my forehead, I whispered, "Arik, stop. I've got a job to do."

"Yeah. Part of that job is searching out the truth." His voice softened. "Bethany doesn't get that, but you do."

Quiet fell, an awkward, uncomfortable lack of sound, and I pushed up from the bed, moving over to the window to stare outside at the slowly falling rain. I was about ready to tell him that I needed to go when he broke the silence.

"I'm sorry," he murmured. "I didn't mean to turn this into something about the case. I've spent most the night thinking about you...about us."

"There isn't an us," I said automatically.

"You and I both know that's a lie." His tone changed, now gruff, low and heated. He sounded the way he did when he was inside me. "There is an us. There's something between us, and you know it." A moment of silence, and then he continued, "I want there to be even *more* between us." He paused again, then asked softly, "Do you want that?"

I closed my eyes, tried to ignore everything that his words made me feel. "Arik..."

"Don't think about our jobs, the case, any of that. We can figure that out, Dena. Just answer the question. Do you want it or not?"

I wanted it so badly that I hurt. And I was tired of denying it.

"Yes."

"Then we'll figure this out," he said. The tension in his voice told me just how much that single word meant to him. "Go to work. I'll talk to you later." A beat of silence. "And I'll think about you all day."

The call ended even while I was still shivering from that last sentence. It was strange, how freeing it had been to admit that. I let that feeling soak into me as I showered and got ready for work.

Yes, I wanted to find out what was going on between Arik and me. I wanted to see where it was going, and what might come of it. He'd been right to tell me to focus on that and not the job before I answered. My dream job that was turning into my nightmare, a fact I had to accept now as my steps slowed to a halt outside the all-too familiar building.

Staring up at the imposing structure, I could feel the bagel I'd eaten turning to a stone in my belly, the coffee becoming acid.

I was going to end up with an ulcer.

"Six months," I told myself. I'd have an ulcer within six months if things didn't change.

I thought about all the times I tried to talk to Bethany about things I'd noticed about this case, about the report Dunne had filed, and how she'd just brushed it off.

What would happen if Arik found evidence of Leayna's innocence? What would happen then? Would Bethany have a way of making it disappear just so she didn't have to admit that she'd indicted the wrong person?

A burning sensation settled mid-center of my chest and I had to force myself to take the first stair. After that, it got easier. As I ascended, I gave myself a mental pep talk. The one good thing about this mess with Pierce was that I wouldn't have to deal with the two of them as much. The paralegals were easier to get along with. Maybe I could do some more digging into Leayna with my time too. If Arik was that convinced of her innocence, there had to be something to prove it, right?

Walking down the hallway, though, it took only one minute to have my mood go from cautiously optimistic to straight down into the bowels of hell. I couldn't even call what I was feeling now pessimistic.

I was feeling downright nauseated and it took everything I had not to throw up as Bethany continued to speak.

Pierce was cleaning out his desk, not looking at me, although the back of his neck was red. Under his designer suit, his broad shoulders were rigid and he moved in jerky motions. I wouldn't have been surprised to see him erupt at any second.

Bethany continued to talk in cool, concise tones as I stared at Pierce, unable to believe what I was hearing, unable to believe he was putting up with this shit.

Finally, Bethany stopped speaking and lifted an eyebrow, a pleased expression on her face. "You've been awfully quiet, Dena. Don't you have anything to say?"

I opened my mouth, then closed it. I wasn't sure it was smart to say what was going through my head at the moment. I needed time to think things through. She started to smirk. Slowly, I angled my gaze back to her.

"Yes, Bethany. As a matter of fact, there is something I'd like to say."

Pierce tensed, his hands tightening on the files he held. Bethany's features froze.

I ignored her, focusing completely on the man who had yet to speak a single word in his defense. "Are you really going to let her do this, Pierce?"

I stared at him hard, and his cheeks flushed. Finally, he shot a look up at me, and I couldn't have imagined that glint of temper in his eyes. Anger burned there, but it wasn't directed at me.

Bethany cut in, "Perhaps if you hadn't done something stupid, and filed a report—"

"I'm done with playing, Bethany." The cold, sharp bite of my voice surprised even me. "We all know I didn't make a move on Pierce, and that I haven't acted unprofessionally with him. There was no way I'd let that go on my record, so *yes*, I filed a counter-complaint. If you think I should have let it go, then you haven't been paying attention to the kind of person I am."

She started to tap her foot, a small foot shod in pink Prada. *A predator in Prada.* Arik had called that right.

"You might be able to throw your weight around with him." I jerked my chin toward Pierce. He'd stopped gathering up his personal belongings and stood there, rigid and unblinking. "But that won't work with me."

Her eyes were cold, assessing. Deciding to ignore her, I gave her my back and focused on Pierce.

"You did good work when we were putting those briefs together, Pierce. I've seen some of the others you've drafted for her. I think you're probably a good lawyer. She's got no right doing this to you." I shook my head. "Is she *really* that good in bed?"

A weird choking noise escaped him, and I wondered if he was trying not to laugh.

Bethany took a step toward me. "That's quite enough."

"Well, you've already complained that I'm unprofessional." Giving her a saccharine smile, I offered, "You want to write me up on that, go ahead, but you might want to consider that I'll make sure any inquiries specifically state why I made that statement."

Pierce was no longer the only one in the room with a flushed, angry face. Bethany's shoulders were rigid, her mouth pinched into a tight, small line as she closed the distance between us.

I tensed, wondering if she would finally snap and slap me. Part of me even wished that she would, that I'd have something I could really use against her.

Surprisingly, she just studied me. After a moment, she spoke, but only to address Pierce. "Please finish getting your things together. You need to be out of here within the hour. I don't know how long the investigation will take. Hopefully, you'll be back to work once it's complete."

The smile she gave him made me want to roll my eyes, but I refrained. Pierce looked away, not looking very impressed.

She reached out and laid a hand on his arm. "I'll put in my recommendation. I think you'll just get a warning on your record. More than likely, you'll be back to work within the next couple of weeks."

"Gee, thanks." The words were thick, bitter with irony. He didn't shake off her hand, however.

She pursed her lips and added softly, "That is assuming Dena doesn't decide to press charges. They will talk to her about her claims."

"I'm betting on it." I gave her a hard look. "I'm looking forward to giving them my thoughts on how this all unfolded. From beginning to end."

Her smile wobbled, then fell away entirely.

She made no other attempts to bait either of us over the next three minutes. That's how long it took Pierce to vacate his office. Bethany followed him to the door and closed it behind him. When she turned to look at me, I could tell she was going to say something, but I was ready for her.

She saw the phone I'd pulled out of my pocket and blinked.

The outrage on her face smoothed away like it had never existed. Her eyes cleared, her mouth curved into a perfunctory smile.

"Please don't tell me you feel the need to record everything you and I say. We're coworkers." She took a step toward me, as if she was trying to regain her footing. "Actually, I'm your supervisor. You're supposed to be able to trust me with things."

"Yeah. That'd be nice." I glanced at my phone again, tapped the screen. It was on my email account, not that she knew. Just the possibility that I was keeping a visual record of her behavior had sucked the malicious wind out of her sails.

It wasn't the ideal way to handle this, but I wouldn't let her screw with my career any more than she already had. And since I wasn't actually recording, no one would be able to claim any sort of breach of privilege.

She flicked another look at the phone, and then walked past me. There was an expression of acute dislike on her features, but she kept her face turned away enough that if my phone had been recording, she couldn't have been seen. "As you can imagine, Pierce's suspension came at an inopportune time. We're trying to expedite the trial on Leayna Mance, and now I've lost my co-chair. You'll be taking his place."

Her words hit me like a punch in the chest. I gripped the phone tighter as I sucked in a breath.

I couldn't have heard her right.

"Second chair?" I said softly. A few weeks ago, I would have been delighted. Now...shit.

"Yes." Her blue eyes for hard as she stared at me. "Welcome to the big times, Dena. You're going to trial."

FIVE

DENA

Welcome to the big times, Bethany had said.

The big times could kiss my ass.

When my phone vibrated, signaling the arrival of yet *another* text, I closed my eyes. It wasn't quite noon on a lazy, rainy Sunday and if life had been perfect, I could've maybe responded to one of those texts, asked him to come over. Maybe we could have taken the next step to see if whatever this was between us could be more.

But life wasn't perfect.

Not even when I'd gotten the one thing I thought I wanted.

The autumn rain that had always seemed so comforting was now driving me crazy. I rubbed my hands over my arms. For some reason, I felt trapped inside my apartment. No matter how much I liked to go out, I'd never been the sort of person who got stir-crazy being in one place too long. At the moment, however, I was almost claustrophobic.

Staring out my window at the leaden gray skies, I made myself ignore my phone. Again. But every text, every call I didn't respond to, or that I let go to voicemail, made it that much harder to ignore the next one.

The sight of his name flashing on the screen was like a punch to the gut.

Not that Arik had said anything or done anything to upset me. On the contrary, his texts ranged from teasing to tempting to sly, and despite my miserable outlook on everything at the moment, each one managed to make me smile.

The phone calls that rolled over to voice mail? The same. He left me smiling...right up until the third call. That one had been laced with a bit of an edge. Nothing rude or even close to hurtful, but I knew I was pushing him further and further away with each passing moment.

Not that I could blame him for being annoyed at me. Here I was dodging his calls, and just a few days ago, I'd been giving him grief because he'd asked for my number but hadn't called back. I hadn't even considered that he might've lost it. Now, he was doing what I'd wanted him to do, and I was leaving him hanging without a word of explanation.

I owed him that.

Except I didn't know what to say.

Things had changed?

Things had *really* changed.

And that was simplifying it to the Nth degree.

Wandering back over to my desk, I looked at the case files Bethany had insisted I take home. She'd given me a snide *you need to get up to speed,* and it'd taken all my self-control not to point out that if she hadn't kept me in the dark all this time, I wouldn't have needed to get caught up.

But there hadn't been a point to saying any of it. She would've found a way to make it my fault and possibly take me back off the case. Dodge, blame, make excuses. It was her MO. Basically do everything except take responsibility for her own actions. She just wanted the win, no matter how she got there.

How in the hell she ended up a prosecutor, I wondered. She

should have been an ambulance chaser. Not even a respectable defense attorney like Arik would stoop to the lengths I suspected Bethany had gone to ensure a victory. She was on par with those sleazy dickwads who used every trick in the book to get their own way.

Finally, I settled down on the couch with one of the files and my fourth cup of coffee. I already had notepads and pencils there from earlier. I'd gone through a couple things before needing to get up and stretch my legs. Now, it was time to focus on the report from the medical examiner.

Within just a few minutes of starting the report, I felt myself starting to get a headache. Considering this was supposed to be an open and shut case, the report from the ME was going to have the jury wondering what the hell was going on.

It sure as hell had me wondering.

I wasn't a medical examiner, and I didn't have a lot of experience reading these types of reports, but from where I sat, it cast plenty of doubt on Leayna Mance as the murderer.

Except I was supposed to help Bethany put Leayna behind bars.

If I'd seen this report earlier, I barely would've considered Leayna a suspect at all. Basically, just someone who needed to be talked to and then crossed off the list before we could get down to finding the real killer.

A killer who no one else seemed to be looking for.

I knew nothing I said would be listened to though, especially considering that a witness I wanted to talk to wasn't exactly around to interview about an alternate theory of the crime.

He was sort of, well, dead.

I'd called Dunne to see if he could help me track the guy down. It hadn't been too hard, as it turned out, because the guy had just been fished out of the river.

In pieces.

A couple of detectives were pissed about it, too, since it turned out he'd been a police informant. Dunne was supposed to let me know if it that investigation connected to my case at all. I wasn't holding my breath. Considering the cops had found fifty thousand in cash in the guy's apartment, finding that murderer wouldn't be pleasant.

I could already imagine what Bethany would say if I went to her with any of this. She'd probably theorize that Leayna Mance had paid the guy to kill Mr. Mance, even if I brought up the fact that the guy had been a possible witness to the late Mr. Mance having cheated on his wife. A tenacious prosecutor wasn't necessarily a bad thing, but one who got a theory in their head and never considered any other possibilities might go too far to protect what they thought of as the truth.

Bethany was definitely the latter.

It'd take a literal smoking gun to sway her opinion, and even then I wasn't sure she'd accept anything less than an actual recording of the crime, complete with authentication certification that the recording wasn't a fake. Maybe not even then...

My phone rang again, interrupting my thoughts. I glanced down at it, almost ready to answer it just so I could have one less thing to worry about. This wasn't really the sort of thing I wanted to discuss over the phone, but I couldn't keep avoiding him. And obsessing about it wasn't doing me any good either.

But it wasn't Arik.

Unknown number flashed across the screen. I would've preferred to ignore it, but considering all of the weird shit going on in this case, I didn't want to miss anything important. It could've been Officer Dunne calling from a payphone. There might be a handful of those still left in the city I supposed.

I answered, keeping my voice flat. "Dena Monroe."

On the other end of the line, I heard open-air, but no response.

I noted the time and gave my name again. "This is Dena Monroe. Can I help you?"

The call ended.

Even as a divorce lawyer, I'd had my fair share of this sort of thing. Yeah, my personal number was unlisted, but it didn't take much to track down a number these days.

It also could've been a wrong number. That did happen.

Still, an uneasy feeling tripped its way down my spine, and I set my phone down on the desk. I didn't have any proof, but my gut told me that the call was about this case, that things were definitely not as cut-and-dry as Bethany wanted to make them appear.

Outside, the rain continued to batter my window, and it didn't stop until around mid-afternoon. The cessation of the white noise didn't really help me focus though. A little while later, the sun teased me with a few rays of sunshine, and that was the only sign I needed to get out of the apartment for a while.

As soon as I stepped outside, I saw that I wasn't the only one who'd been going stir crazy. The streets were already bustling, and my destination, the little Indian place on the corner, was packed by the time I got there. The hostess recognized me, giving me a quick smile and pointing to a single table in the corner. Tucking myself into the minuscule space, I had barely sat down when my phone buzzed.

It was Arik.

Again.

I didn't like it, but it was the perfect time to respond. I had an excuse not to answer in any way other than a text. It might've been cowardly of me, but I was okay with that at the moment.

Decision made, I started drafting my text. I was still working on it when the server came by with my usual tea. "Do you want your usual, Dena?"

"Yes." I gave her a distracted smile, my attention on the man I was texting.

As she left, I looked back down at the message, wondering if this was the right thing. He'd told me, made me believe we could have something. Then this mess happened with the case.

Was it over before we even had a chance to figure things out?

I read it again.

Hi, Arik. Sorry I haven't been able to answer your calls. I'm eating right now. Things with the case have gotten a bit complicated, keeping me busy.

We need to talk, but I won't be able to until later this week.

I deliberated a moment and then added,

Thinking of you.

I sent it, then put the phone in my purse, telling myself that I needed to put this out of my head so I could focus on work. We would talk later, once I'd had some time to get my priorities sorted out and had a plan in place.

MONDAY WAS ABOUT AS FAR AWAY from Friday as it could be. It dawned sunny and bright, the sun's light trying to scorch my corneas, teasing the headache that had been nagging me on and off most of the weekend.

I didn't want to be here at all, but there wasn't anything to be done for it. I had to go to work.

I hadn't heard from Arik since a text he'd sent Sunday evening saying that he'd get back to me when he had a time he could talk.

He needed to hurry the hell up.

On the other hand, I needed time to think through what I wanted to say, because I still had absolutely no idea. No idea what to do or say. No idea of what I even really wanted.

Distracted by my thoughts, I didn't even notice the commotion going on outside my office door until I almost ran into one of the maintenance guys on my way in. One who seemed to be carrying things *out* of my office.

What the hell?

"What is this?" I demanded.

He glanced over his shoulder at me. "Cleaning this old place out." He paused, squinting at me. "Are you Ms. Monroe?"

"Yes." Planting one hand on my hip, I stared at him and tried to look intimidating. It was hard to look tough though when you stood five foot nothing, and had a skinny vanilla latte with a double shot of espresso in your hand, but I did my best. "You want to tell me why you're cleaning it out? It happens to be my office."

A part of me hoped that Bethany had just decided to fire me. If she had…I hated the thrill of happiness that went through me. I should've been devastated that I lost the job I'd wanted my whole life.

Before I could get too excited though, the guy spoke again.

"You got a new office." He pointed down the hall and rattled off a number. "Down there."

My heart sank as I realized the office was right next to Pierce. It'd be bigger, but I really didn't want to be any closer to the man than I had to be.

"Okay." I waved a hand at him. "Sorry about getting snippy. I was just surprised. Thank you."

"Don't thank me. Thank your boss." He turned and ambled off, pushing a cart laden with boxes.

I stepped into my office and then looked back down the hall.

"I'll finish up in here, if it's okay with you. Most of it's my personal stuff."

He glanced at me and shrugged as if to say it didn't matter to him one way or the other. I ducked inside the tiny space I'd been using as an office and looked around. It looked like pretty much everything, save for the corkboard and a few other little odds and ends, had already been moved.

Blowing out a breath, I reached for the door behind me.

A hand shot out, and I didn't have time to panic or even think.

Two seconds later, the door was shut and Arik Porter stood in front of me.

"Miss Monroe, I believe you wanted to talk." His voice was calm, even professional.

"What're you doing?" I demanded, gaping at him. "This is—"

That was all I managed to get out before his mouth slammed down over mine.

A hundred indignant questions and statements faded away, replaced by an insatiable, irrational sort of need clawing through me. Arik's thigh pushed between mine, and the flirty, flippy skirt that I'd worn today was no barrier. He kept moving until his knee was pressed directly against me.

He tore his mouth away, nipping at my bottom lip. "Do you know how long it's been since I had you wrapped around my dick, Dena?"

Things inside me twisted.

"I can tell you...far too long."

Shit.

He wasn't kidding. It'd been too long.

I took a deep breath, trying to clear my head. It did no good though, because with it, came the scent of him. Soap and spice and whatever it was that was him.

Fuck.

When he pressed his lips to my neck, I swallowed a whimper, and then he kissed me again.

Greedy, I sucked his tongue into my mouth, and when his body drew tight in response, a primitive sort of victory welled up inside me. I loved that I could do this to this man. This dominant, powerful man.

Arik ran his hands through my hair.

We needed to stop, I thought hazily. This was crazy.

I couldn't bring the words to my lips yet. I wanted him so much.

Cool air caressed my chest, and I realized he'd let go of my hair at some point to start unbuttoning my blouse. If he touched his hands or mouth to my breasts, I'd be gone. There'd be no stopping.

"Stop," I finally managed to say. "Arik, stop...we're not doing this here."

He reached down between us and cupped me, one finger rubbing against my panties. I was already aching and wet for him.

"Are you sure?" he asked, a hot, sweet teasing note in his voice.

I bit my lower lip to muffle my moan as his fingers pressed against me. He backed me up against the door and leaned into me, his body hard in all the right places.

In the sane, rational part of my mind that wasn't already completely undone by him, a voice whispered, *You're in your office. You're supposed to be meeting with Bethany soon. You can't do this.*

Bethany.

Office.

Dammit all to hell.

I caught his wrist and dragged his hand away. "No, Arik."

They were the hardest two words I'd ever had to say.

Against my lips, he murmured, "No?"

Feeling the edges of my control fracturing, I forced my hands between us and shoved at his chest. "No."

He took a step back, his expression wild for a single moment before he brought himself back under control.

Voice shaking, I gestured toward the hall. "Bethany McDermott might think it's just fine to screw around on the job, but I don't. I'm not doing this here."

Arik held up his hands to show that he was backing off. "You're right. I'm sorry." He scraped his fingertips down his jaw, scratching at the stubble already darkening his chin. "I...Dena, you make me lose my mind a little. I'm sorry."

He meant it, I could tell.

"If we're working, we can't do this. We can't work if we do this sort of thing." *We might not work anyway.* The thought flitted through my head. Looking away, I pushed a shaky hand through my hair to smooth it down. Taking a deep breath, I forced my gaze back to his. I had to tell him. I'd waited too long. "Listen, Arik, about the case—" The shrill sound of the phone on my desk interrupted me. Feeling drained already, I moved toward it and picked it up. "Dena Monroe."

"We're meeting in fifteen. You've got a decent office now, so use it. Get your ass together." Bethany's voice, flat and emotionless, barked out of the receiver. I had no chance to respond before she hung up. Still, as I lowered the phone into the cradle, I snapped a sarcastic little salute.

"The queen has spoken." Arik said, his voice dry. I looked back just in time to see him run a hand through his hair, settling it into place. He adjusted his tie and the lapels of his jacket. Just like that, he looked like he had just stepped off the cover of GQ Lawyerly.

Me, on the other hand? I needed to swing by the ladies'

room and make judicious use of one of the stalls, otherwise I'd get to walk around with damp panties for the rest of the day. I was sure Arik would've loved that, but it wasn't something I planned on sharing. Of course, I also needed to touch up my lipstick since smudge-proof wasn't really much protection when it came to Arik's kisses. Then I had to brace myself to deal with Bethany.

Fifteen minutes wouldn't be nearly enough time for that, but I had a feeling it was all I'd get. What I wasn't going to be able to do was tell him the one thing he needed to know.

Shit.

I paused with my hand on the door. "I'll go first." I glanced up at him. "When can we talk?"

"I was thinking about tonight. I'd like to take you out for dinner."

I closed my eyes. Dinner. It sounded like a date, wonderful, really. But it also sounded like a terrible idea at the same time, and if I was smart I would've been thinking up ways to explain that to him. There were a thousand reasons why going out tonight would be a bad idea, and yet I couldn't think of a single one that would make sense without a much longer discussion.

I opened the door and stepped out. A part of me breathed a sigh of relief when I was able to slip into the bathroom before Arik emerged. I took as little time as possible, hoping it was enough time for Arik to have left, but he was still in the hall when I stepped out.

I suppressed a scowl as he came over to me. I wanted to demand that he leave, but he gave me a polite smile and started talking.

"Ms. Monroe, I'd like to thank you for the advice on the divorce attorney," Arik said, head bent toward mine. His voice was brisk, business-like. "I'll take those recommendations to my friend. I'm sure she'll appreciate it as well."

"Ah, yes." I swallowed. "Of course. No...no trouble at all." I felt like I was rambling. Did I need to say anything else?

He stopped walking and I did the same, looking up at him. He held out a hand. Befuddled, I reached out and he shook my hand once, twice. Just a nice, professional handshake, nothing strange here.

It was one of the most surreal things I'd ever experienced.

"Dena...oh, and I see you two have already found each other. Excellent."

At the sound of Bethany's voice, my blood chilled. My smile froze on my face.

Shit. Shit. Shit.

She drew closer as I let go of Arik's hand. Her eyes slid all over him and a stab of jealousy went through me. I would've hated anyone looking at him like that. It being Bethany was so much worse.

"Feeling out the opposition already, Miss Monroe?" She jerked a hand toward my office. "I was just heading your way. Let's go to your new office, shall we?"

She turned, the indication that I should trail along behind her like a disobedient child very clear.

Then I realized she hadn't only been speaking to me.

She'd been speaking to Arik, too.

Was he here...?

Oh. Oh, *shit*. This was what I got for dodging his phone calls all weekend.

"You're here for a meeting, aren't you?" I asked, my voice low as I started to follow Bethany.

He glanced my way, then nodded, his expression puzzled.

I really should have just blurted it out earlier, but it was too late now. It was time to face the music.

SIX

ARIK

Dena made me into a complete moron. I still couldn't believe I had almost pushed her up against the wall and sank my dick inside her, right there in the middle of the cubicle that had been her office.

I completely lost my mind around her. That's all there was to it.

And I loved it. I couldn't deny it.

Everything about her, from the way she submitted to the way she fought, the way she responded as a Dominant in her own right, how she gave as well as she took. All of it challenged me.

But I was going to have to be a lot more careful. She was right. What I'd almost done had been beyond stupid, beyond irresponsible. It wouldn't have only ruined me if we'd been caught, it could've destroyed Dena's career. It didn't matter what Bethany did. If she'd caught Dena and me together, she'd have made sure Dena paid for it.

Slanting a look over at Dena, I opened my mouth to say something. I didn't even know what I'd been planning to say, because whatever it was died as I caught sight of her pale, strained face.

Her mouth was drawn into a tight line, and I wondered if maybe she hadn't been feeling well over the weekend. She'd avoided my calls, or at least it seemed that way, despite her text where she insisted she'd been busy. Granted, I wouldn't have put it past Bethany to dump a shitload of work on her ADAs at the last minute just so she could go out on the town. It wasn't like Bethany was exactly known for her work ethic. That was practically common knowledge at this point.

I wanted to pull Dena aside, ask her if she was okay, but there was no time for it. And no place.

Bethany led us to a door and pulled out a key, but instead of unlocking it, she turned the key over to Dena. "It's yours, after all. You should be the first one to go in."

"Well, besides the maintenance people who moved me in, of course." Dena's tone was perfectly level, but Bethany and I both heard the bite.

Bethany's sapphire eyes flashed, but when she saw me looking, she just laughed. "Like we'd make *you* do all that heavy lifting, Dena. You could break a nail...or your back, as tiny as you are. We wouldn't want that, would we?"

I wiggled my jaw, recalling the strength Dena had in her small frame. Somehow I didn't think hefting a few boxes would do her any harm.

Dena unlocked the door and stepped inside, flicking on the lights. From where I stood, I could tell that it was just the typical office any ADA would get, but as I watched, Dena's shoulders rose, then fell on a breath that seemed more than a little unsteady. She stepped to the side quickly, allowing Bethany and me to enter. I waited for Bethany and she lingered, her gaze drifting over me. I resisted the urge to curl my lip.

I didn't mind a woman finding me attractive, but there was

something about how Bethany looked at me that made me think of one of those female insects who ate the males after mating.

Moving toward the desk and the two miserable chairs in front of it, I looked around. "Where's your other ADA? Lawton, right?"

Bethany had probably sent him out to get donuts already.

She gave me a sharp smile, as though she'd caught that last thought. "I haven't had a chance to eat anything today." She gave Dena a dazzling smile. "I'm sure Arik is also hungry. Why don't you run to the deli on the corner and grab something for us? You can get it this time, can't you? I'll get it next time."

"No need." I gave them both a pleasant smile as I sat. "I ordered a dozen bagels and coffee for four on my way in. It's being delivered. We've got maybe five minutes. I'm sure the delivery person will be able to find us, right?"

Bethany's eyes went frosty for a split second before she smiled at me. That smile didn't reach her eyes. It rarely did. "How kind of you, Arik. Although we won't need the fourth coffee. I didn't get around to notifying anybody outside my office, but Pierce Lawton has been temporarily reassigned. He'll be back in a few days, but Dena has been made second chair."

Dena.

It hit me almost like a physical blow.

I turned my head and stared at her.

The case had gotten complicated. Wasn't that what she said in her text?

Complicated?

That was a hell of an understatement.

"Dena might like that fourth coffee, though," Bethany said, chattering on like any one of us actually gave a fuck about an extra coffee. "She seems to have something of a caffeine addiction, I'm afraid."

"It's either coffee or the blood of my enemies, Bethany."

Dena gave a tight smile without looking my way. "Coffee seems the safest option."

I was still looking at her. Only when I sensed Bethany staring at me did I look away, forcing myself to meet Bethany's gaze.

"I assure you," Bethany said, smiling prettily. "She looks young and inexperienced, but I've been watching her. She's got a sharp mind. She'll do fine."

"I've no doubt." I was surprised how even I managed to keep my voice.

Second chair.

She'd known. All fucking weekend.

I could tell by the way she wouldn't look at me that this hadn't come as a surprise.

She'd known when we'd been in her office, dammit. Not even ten minutes ago, and she hadn't said anything.

How could this be happening?

A million things raged inside me, but my game face was exceptional, as always. I managed a nonchalant air as I put my briefcase on my lap and opened it.

"We need to get down to brass tacks, don't we? I want to talk about the break-in, among other things."

"The break-in has nothing to do with anything." Bethany waved a dismissive hand. "Mrs. Mance lives in a nice neighborhood. I heard she had some pretty expensive pieces of art. Somebody probably wanted to make some money."

"Your average thug wouldn't know a Picasso from a postage stamp, Bethany." I slapped a list of the destroyed pieces on the desk. She'd settled down behind it despite the fact that it was supposed to be Dena's office. "All the damaged pieces seem to be accounted for. Nothing was stolen. Just...destroyed."

"It's still not related to this case."

"We don't know that," Dena said from off to my side.

I resisted the urge to look at her.

"We do." Bethany gave her a cold look that made my hands curl into fists. "There is *no* evidence connecting the two events. No reason for anyone to ransack Ms. Mance's house. Unless, of course, she was trying for sympathy. Or maybe an insurance scam."

"She has no reason to do that," I said through gritted teeth. I wasn't sure which was pissing me off more, Bethany's treatment of Dena or her attitude toward Leayna.

"Money's always a motive. If her late husband had been planning on divorcing her..."

"She doesn't have any money issues," Dena neatly interrupted as she pulled a file out of a box and put a report down on the desk in front of Bethany. "I had a source look into it."

I saw a real flicker of surprise on Bethany's face. "You were able to follow up on quite a bit this weekend."

Maybe Dena really had been busy.

Dena started to say something else, but Bethany cut her off, dismissing her as she focused on me. "We have a solid case against Mrs. Mance, Arik. She'd be wise to just plead out."

I took a second to make sure my voice was calm. "My client is innocent."

There was a knock at the door.

Dena answered while Bethany glared at me. The cute college coed who bustled in, handing out coffee and depositing the box of bagels ended up hurrying out as quickly as possible. I hoped the twenty-dollar tip would make up for the tension in the air.

Dena seemed unaffected, but I knew better. She stood at the window, staring outside as she slowly stirred cream and sugar into her coffee.

Absently, I noted the cup on the desk. Skinny vanilla latte. Next time, I told myself.

Next time... What in the hell? Why was I thinking about the next time? Or coffee? Or anything other than the fact that she'd hidden something pretty damn important from me?

And why was I thinking about any of this when I had a case to focus on? A client whose life was on the line.

"Mrs. Mance really should make a deal," Bethany said, her voice even. "None of this is going away."

With that, she stood up, selected a bagel and took a coffee. As she started to walk out, I focused on Dena.

No way in hell would I just let this go. If I walked out of this office, I had no way of knowing when I'd get to talk to her again.

"I'll need your ADA for a little while this morning. I'm sure you're...busy, Bethany, but my client needs to get a few things from her house, and I'm sure you'll want somebody from the DA's office there." Rising, I looked back at her. "To make sure everything's done by the book, of course."

Bethany paused, studying me. Then she shrugged. "Just make sure you don't keep her long. She's needed here."

Shifting my gaze to Dena, I picked up my briefcase.

"Let's go."

I wasn't waiting to have that talk.

And I sure as hell wasn't making that a request.

.

SEVEN

What I wanted to do was tell Arik that I'd meet him at Leayna's, but it didn't make sense for us to take separate cabs, especially since the first one had been so hard to get.

When we stopped a block short of the Mance address, I looked around. Not that parking was easy anywhere in the city, but I didn't think we were going to be walking from here.

The luxury high-rise in front of us hadn't yet opened for general viewing, but real estate agents and businesses were making grabs for prime spots.

But that didn't explain why we'd parked here.

"What are we doing?" I asked as we rolled to a stop.

"Talking."

I didn't bother to play dumb and point out that he'd said we were going to his client's house. I'd known it was bullshit from the second the words left his mouth. It was strange how well I seemed to know him already.

"This place isn't open to the public. How are we...?"

The words stopped as a man came rushing up to the cab door, opening it with a wide smile. "Mr. Porter, it's great to see you, sir. Coming by to see how the construction's going? I hear the penthouse will be ready soon."

"Before Thanksgiving," Arik said easily as he shook hands with the other man. "My father said he ran into a few snags with some permits. He's still learning the differences between building codes in Chicago and New York."

His father?

What the hell?

"If this one does well, do you think your family will continue expanding here?"

His family?

Arik nodded without looking at me. "That's the plan."

"Well, sir, we really appreciate the jobs around here." The man opened the front door. "You and your friend take your time. The building inspector's not due for another few hours."

Arik thanked him and stepped inside, seemingly waiting for me to ask. I didn't because I'd already connected enough dots to construct a decent picture. Defense attorneys made damn good money – or they could.

But it sounded like Arik was already loaded. Family money, even if he hadn't gone into the family business.

Part of me wondered why that was, but I didn't ask. We had enough to deal with without adding family into the mix. Maybe, eventually...I shook my head. No use even attempting to think that far ahead.

Neither of us said a word as we rode up to the top floor, then walked down a dimly lit hall. It was clear that even though things looked completed, there was still a bit more that needed to be done.

It was all black, white and chrome, completely masculine. As Arik locked the door behind us, I looked at the modern fixtures and then over at him. "This place doesn't suit you."

"No." He paced over toward me, crossing his arms over his

chest, his emerald green eyes narrowed. "I'm not here to discuss my future accommodations, though. Why didn't you tell me?"

I didn't have to ask what he was talking about. "I was going to," I said. Averting my face, I blew out a breath. "As soon as I figured out how."

"It would have been easy. All you had to do was answer one of my calls, or one of my texts, instead of blowing me off." Biting anger underscored his voice, but I couldn't really blame him. "Look at me."

When I didn't, he shot a hand into my hair.

He. Did. Not.

I jerked against his hold, glaring at him. "Let go."

"And not just blowing me off, but doing it to figure out how to put an innocent woman in jail."

He still hadn't let go of my hair and my scalp was starting to tingle from the pressure, but not in a good way.

"*I* spent the weekend getting caught up on a case that had been assigned to me by my direct superior." Rising up on my toes, I shoved my face into his. "And if you don't let go of my hair *right* now, this discussion is through and this so-called *relationship* is through."

Something flickered through his eyes and slowly he let go. Tension radiated off of him, and for the first time since I'd met him, I was thoroughly aware of just how much larger he was than me. More than a foot taller, broad shoulders, muscled torso...

"I'm sorry," he said, his voice strangely gentle. "I just—"

"I found out on Thursday morning," I cut him off. "Bethany has been fucking with me almost from the get-go, and then she throws Pierce under the bus, claiming he made some bullshit unofficial complaint about how I acted unprofessionally and made an advance on him. None of it happened, of course, and we all knew it. He stood there and let her say it, knowing it was all crap." Now that I'd started, it all came pouring out. "I filed a formal complaint against him and told her I'd be happy to explain in detail everything that's happened since I started. He ended up getting suspended while they investigate him. So that meant I became second chair."

Arik was the one looking away now.

My lips trembled. I could feel the tears threatening, and it pissed me off. I didn't want to cry. I never wanted to cry. I wanted to yell at him. I was angry and hurt. And too much had happened in the past couple months for me to be able to handle it.

Turning away, I sniffed and reached up to press my finger-tips under my eyes as I tried to hold the tears at bay.

"Dena..." Arik's voice was hoarse.

I heard him coming up behind me. I started to shake my head, tried to step away from him, but I was too slow.

He was already wrapping one arm around my hips, his palm pressing to my belly while the other came up and covered my throat. The gesture should've been threatening, oppressive, but for me, feeling the strength of him was comforting. Safe.

"Don't do that," he whispered against the top of my head. "I'm...fuck, baby, I'm sorry. This is messing with my head. I told you that I couldn't think straight around you."

"You're an asshole," I snapped. Then I sniffled, taking the sting out of my statement. "I told you getting involved was a bad idea."

He pressed his lips to my hair, his thumb making circles over my pulse. I told myself I needed to pull away, end this.

That was what I needed to do.

So why was I letting him turn me around and tip my face up?

Why was I letting him kiss me?

Why was I letting him push his hands into my hair? He

unerringly sought out the areas of my scalp that ached a bit and massaged, his touch tender rather than rough.

I moaned into his mouth. When his teeth gently scored my lower lip, I whimpered, and without letting myself think about the stupidity of what we were doing, I placed my hands on his chest and slowly slid them up, shoving his jacket back.

He shrugged out of it, and while I fumbled with his tie, he pulled up my skirt. My hips jerked as he ripped off my panties and I gasped into his mouth. I fumbled with his shirt, desperate to feel him. He tore at his belt, and then he boosted me up, his need fueling my own.

I gasped as he thrust inside me, holding me up in the middle of that cold, sterile room that didn't suit him at all. I wrapped my legs around his waist as his cock stretched and burned. I wasn't ready, and it hurt, but when he would have waited, I rocked against him, urging him on.

His eyes burned into mine, desperation in the depths. "We shouldn't do this," he said, his voice harsh. I could feel his body trembling. "I do the stupidest things with you, Dena."

"Me, too." I tugged his face closer, kissing him, exploring his mouth with mine.

We said nothing else. In the middle of that room, with him holding me, I rode him. It was slow, almost torturous, as I used my inner muscles to squeeze him. His hands gripped my ass and I wound my arm around his neck, the two of us moving together in a way that I could never be with anyone else.

He felt huge inside me, my weight driving me down on his cock until I was so full of him that I didn't know where he ended and I began. The sensations were almost too much and every muscle in my body trembled, but I held on.

The room began to whirl around us, then my vision focused and I realized it wasn't the room moving, but us. Arik took two strides, putting my back to the wall before he caught my knees, and began to hammer into me. Each driving thrust pulled a moan from me, and before I knew it, he had pounded me straight into orgasm.

He came a moment later, his groan smothered against my throat even as he pulsed inside me, the feeling enough to trigger a second, smaller climax.

We stayed like that for a couple silent minutes. I could feel an internal clock ticking in my head as his weight continued to spread my thighs. Muscles strained and I started to feel all of the aches that came from being thoroughly fucked.

A deep sigh escaped him, then slowly, he eased me to the ground. I sucked in a breath as he pulled out, my pussy throbbing with the sudden loss.

As he tugged his trousers up, I stepped around him. A black silk scrap lay on the floor. Face flushed, I picked it up and moved over to the kitchen area. I hoped the water was on. I was wet, his semen leaking down my thighs. Thankfully, the water was indeed on, and I quickly wiped myself, using the destroyed remains of my panties.

When I turned, Arik was staring outside.

Good. I wasn't ready to look at him. Or myself. I flushed with shame.

So much for respecting my office and not having sex on the job. I was such a hypocrite.

Throat tight, I smoothed my hands down my skirt and looked toward the door. I took one shaking step, then another. My purse and briefcase waited there, on the floor. I didn't even remember putting them down.

"Dena. We need to talk," Arik said. He sounded tired now.

He couldn't be any more tired than me.

"No," I said softly. "I've said everything I needed to say. I'm just trying to do my job, you know." Now I glanced back at him, myriad emotions churning inside. "All I ever wanted to do was be a prosecutor. This was supposed to be my dream job and it's become a nightmare. Everything went to shit with Bethany. So, yeah, I took a few days to come to grips with how things changed last week. I needed time, Arik. That's who I am. You're pissed off about it. Fine."

"That's...dammit, Dena!" He started toward me.

I held up my hands. "Don't. I'm not ready to talk about this now. I have a job to do, and it doesn't involve getting fucked on the taxpayer's dime. Dammit!" My voice broke. "I'm no better than she is."

"That's not...Dena!"

Grabbing my bag and briefcase, I hurried through the door and practically ran for the elevator. He was right behind me, but as I darted inside the elevator, I looked at him. "Don't, Arik. I can't do this right now. I mean it."

He stopped, but I could see how much it cost him to do nothing. The pain on his face nearly destroyed my resolve, but what I'd done was still too clear in my mind.

I let the doors close.

I ate lunch while I was out.

Well, it was sort of lunch. I didn't think that a giant pile of French fries and a milkshake *really* counted as food, but I needed comfort in the worst way, and I wasn't in the mood to talk to anyone. Even my friends.

I'd done the stupidest thing imaginable. No, I hadn't realized Arik was a defense attorney right off the bat, but once I *had* known, I should have ended things, period. Completely and totally.

But I hadn't.

I could do it now, but I didn't want to.

I let myself brood over that for a short while as I splurged on my sugary, salty, junk food lunch, and then I made one more stop before heading back to my office.

I had to get new underwear.

There were flowers on the table by the door when I arrived back in my new office. Knowing it was probably rude, but past the point of caring, I took them to the nearest trash can and threw them out. I was allergic anyway. I left the vase sitting on a long table just outside my office. I had no idea who the flowers came from, but I left a note inside my office. *No flowers, please. Allergies.*

Not even five minutes passed before the phone rang.

Massaging my temples, I closed my eyes as I answered, "Dena Monroe."

There was a brief pause, then Bethany's voice, far more friendly and warm than I'd ever heard from her, came over the line. "Good afternoon, Dena. I was just wondering how you're settling into your new office."

The tone threw me off balance for a moment, but I was too used to her personality to be lured in by a couple of kind words. Besides, I was a lawyer. People changed their faces in this business as often as they changed their underwear. Probably more in some cases.

I flushed at the thought of underwear and forced aside the memories that quickly followed.

Tapping my pen against the blotter on my desk, I opened my eyes and stared at the mostly empty calendar. "It's fine, thank you. Is there something you need?"

"No – well, yes. I was wondering if you'd like to join me for lunch. We could go over what you learned at Mrs. Mance's apartment."

"I picked up lunch on the way back, but I can tell you what I learned. Nothing. He was just there to pick up a few personal effects for Mrs. Mance, just like he said." I lied without batting an eyelash. "We didn't talk much."

That wasn't a lie.

The connection between us buzzed, followed by a high-pitched noise that was like an icepick in my already aching head.

"Was there anything else, Bethany?" I asked, determined now to get off the phone. I needed to take something for this damn headache and get to work. Maybe then I wouldn't think so much about everything that happened today. Or the past several days.

"No," she responded, her voice cooler now, as short and sharp as I'd come to expect from her.

Maybe I hadn't been as appreciative of her olive branch as I was supposed to have been.

Oh, well. Of all the things I'd fucked up recently, that was near the bottom of my list.

"Okay, then." I hung up without another word and grabbed my purse. I dry-swallowed a couple of over-the-counter painkillers and focused on the files on my desk.

Work.

I'd just focus on work.

HOURS LATER, I threw my pen down and shoved back from the desk.

I didn't know how many phone calls I'd made, but it hadn't made a difference. I hadn't been able to find any motive for murder. No affairs, no money issues...at least nothing on her side. The victim, however, he'd been far from squeaky clean. I didn't have anything substantial, but there was definitely more to his story than anyone had said.

Then there were the forensics.

Leayna couldn't have killed her husband. There was no way.

The crime scene reports showed that no blood or fibers or anything had been found in the sinks, bathroom drains, or anywhere else in their home. She would have had to wrap herself completely up, including her face, and dispose of what-ever she'd worn during the attack.

All before the cops arrived.

Before Arik had gotten there.

I tried calling the cops to ask if they'd done a search of the dumpsters and trash cans within a mile or so of her home, but they said they'd been instructed that such a procedure wasn't necessary.

When I'd asked why, they'd told me to talk to my boss.

"I'm second chair on this case. That means following up on this very line is my job, Detective," I'd said, pacing the room as I continued to talk into my Bluetooth.

"You're basically an errand girl," the detective on the other end had said, clearly disinterested. "Lawton was the errand boy, now you're the errand girl. Why don't you take it easy and wait for your boss to tell you to fetch some donuts or something? Leave the detective work to the professionals."

He hung up then.

I'd debated over it long and hard, and had finally decided that while it would be fulfilling to talk to Detective Dumbass' superior, it wouldn't have been the *wise* thing.

I'd been here only a short while, and had already filed one complaint. It had been justified, yes, but word got around. I didn't want to become known as the woman who was constantly making problems. Even if there were actual issues. The more I made of each problem, the worse they'd become.

There were real problems with this case, but since Bethany refused to pay attention, and it seemed that the cops weren't all that interested, I'd have to continue to see what I could dig up.

The good little lawyer in me reminded me that I needed to update my superior.

The good little lawyer needed to shut the hell up and leave me alone, but I didn't see that happening any time soon.

So, grudgingly, I packed everything up, save for the few notes I'd kept in my notebook. I did most everything digitally, but sometimes I just focused better if I wrote things out.

The notes I held were the bits and pieces of the case that didn't add up.

I'd hoped that if I wrote them down, I could find some magical way to make them make sense, or some string that would connect them that I just hadn't seen yet. That miracle hadn't yet occurred.

The holes were obvious, too, so I was going to show everything to Bethany, and then head on out.

That was the plan, anyway.

When I stepped out into the hallway, an almost ghostly silence greeted me. It was nearly seven, but I hadn't noticed it until that moment when I flicked a look at my phone and saw the time glowing up at me. The lights had been dimmed in the lower corridors, and I sighed as I hurried toward the stairs. Bethany wasn't buried down here in the tombs liked the rest of us plebes, so I had to walk through several equally darkened hallways to reach her.

I knew they did it to conserve energy, but I didn't really like walking down dimly-lit corridors of mostly empty buildings. Especially cavernous ones that made every step echo.

I spent far too much time watching zombie shit, I thought as I made my way down the corridor to Bethany's office. She might not even be here. It was way past the time somebody as important as *Bethany McDermott* would work. Especially when she had such a capable ADA to help her.

Smirking, I shook my head.

And then a sound caught my ears.

Oh, for crying out loud.

Those low grunts, the moaning.

She was like a fucking cat in heat.

Immediately, though, I flushed in self-reprisal. Had I really been any better? So I hadn't done it in my office. Did that really make a difference?

I paused outside her office, glancing toward the window automatically.

She hadn't even completely closed the blinds. It was like she almost *wanted* to be caught.

I guessed that meant Pierce hadn't stayed that mad at her, because there they were, Bethany bent face down over her desk, while he stood behind her...

Wait.

That wasn't Pierce.

The man bent down and fisted a hand in her hair, yanking roughly as he pulled her up high enough for me to see more of her breasts than I wanted to.

She whimpered, her face screwed up as a passionate moan escaped her. By contrast, the guy slamming into her looked detached. Almost disinterested. Then he straightened, and I found myself staring at his face.

He had a cold face, sharply cut with long, hollow cheeks, and a mouth that might be considered sexy. But he was...cold.

To say the least.

Shivering, I backed away, moving far more silently than I had earlier.

I didn't know why, but I didn't want them to know I was there. And it had nothing to do with Bethany and everything to do with that man.

For the first time in my life, a man truly scared the shit out of me.

NINE

DENA

I made two stops on the way home.

After the day I'd had, I needed two things: sushi and sake.

I placed the order for sushi from my mobile before getting on the subway, and after I picked it up, I hit the liquor store and got a bottle of sake. Unsurprisingly, the guy behind the counter carded me, then hit on me when he saw I was twenty-six.

I was going to have to show some serious willpower not to overindulge and show up to work hungover tomorrow.

Juggling my food, liquor, and briefcase as I rode the elevator up, I barely heard the buzz of my phone.

My heart leaped. Stupid of me, but every time it had done that today, I thought it might be Arik. Yes, I told him I needed time and I did, but that didn't mean I wasn't thinking about him. Constantly.

Once inside, I emptied my arms as quickly as possible, and then grabbed my phone, but it had already stopped ringing.

The call log showed a missed call alright, but it had been from Bethany. Boss Bitch had called nearly an hour after I'd seen her fucking some guy – or rather some guy fucking *her* over the desk in her office. I had to push the catty thoughts out of my

head, though. I'd lost the right to get all snide and conde-
scending on that one when I'd let Arik fuck me on the clock.

Did the location really matter?

Not so much in my mind.

The phone buzzed a moment later, signaling an incoming
text.

As her name came up, I sighed, then forced myself to read
the message.

Came by your office, needed to discuss a few pertinent
details about the case with you. You weren't there. Did you
leave already?

I fought the urge to hurl the phone. I hated how much she
screwed with my temper. I was usually a level-headed person,
but Bethany brought out the worst in me.

I didn't even want to think about what Arik brought out
in me.

Before I could say something stupid, I grabbed a piece of
paper and scrawled down all the mean things I wanted to say,
and then I shot her back a quick, professional response.

I left about an hour ago. I didn't think you'd still be there.
Sorry. Can it wait until tomorrow or should I call?

There. Nothing like the *bite me, bitch* that I wanted to say.

It can wait, of course. See you in the morning.

After reading the text, I turned off my phone, something
that might end up causing problems if anything important
happened during the night, but I was the second chair, not the
ADA actually trying the case. That's why they paid her more.

Once that was done, I got my sushi and my sake and flopped
down on the couch.

A few minutes for myself, I thought. I just wanted a few
minutes for myself.

SILKEN, warm water lapped against my skin.

Arik's strong arms wrapped around me.

His lips slid down my neck, and I sighed in pleasure as the jets from the tub had the water frothing all around us.

"This case doesn't make sense," I told him.

"Don't talk about the case." Arik caught my ear between his teeth and bit down. "Take a few minutes for yourself."

For myself? I looked down at the bubbling water, at the tanned arm that held me tight against a hard body. "Isn't that what this is?"

He chuckled. "This is part of it. But even now, you're thinking about the case. About everything that isn't right. Think about the things that *are* right."

"And what's that?" I demanded, my voice sharp.

He slid his hands up my belly to cup my breasts. I moaned, writhing against him.

"You're with me now." He palmed my breasts and pinched my nipples. They tightened and he ran his tongue along the rim of my ear.

"I–" Shaking my head, I looked up at him. Water rushed over the sides of the tub and I couldn't see him.

I didn't know where we were.

"I'm not sure if it's right or not. We needed to talk to—"

Arik kissed me, his tongue stabbing deep into my mouth. The hands that had been stroking my breasts moved. One going to my hair, and the other to my hip, gripping me and pulling me in tight against his cock.

The water...

It was gone.

So was the bathtub and the bathroom.

We were in one of the rooms at Club Privé, and when I tore my mouth from Arik's to look around, I saw Carrie and Gavin sitting at a small, round table in the corner.

"What are you doing here?" I demanded.

"Making sure you don't break the rules again," my best friend said, tipping the glass toward me. She nodded over to the side. "Those two are all about breaking the rules, but you're not, Dena. You're a good girl."

"I am not." I glared at her, trying to make sense of the conversation even as I tried to figure out who she was talking about. One quick look told me. It was Bethany and the guy she'd been with. His face – it nagged me. Harsh, handsome and cold. "Who *is* he?"

"Trouble." Arik kissed the middle of my breastbone, easing my arched back over his arm. "You know who he is, or you wouldn't see him here. He's trouble. Stay away from him."

"It's not like I was going to ask him to join us," I snapped.

"Good. I don't share." Arik went to his knees in front of me, pressing his mouth to the midline of my torso before starting down my stomach.

"Why are those two in my club, darling?" Gavin asked, gesturing to Bethany and her companion.

Two of the security guards pulled them away from each other, then dragged them away, still naked.

Carrie answered Gavin's question, "Ask Dena. She's the reason we're all here."

"I'm...no." Shaking my head, I tried to get my bearings, but couldn't.

Not with Arik's lips brushing against the sensitive skin between my thighs.

Carrie and Gavin watched, almost curiously. "He has good technique," Carrie said softly.

I moaned, hardly able to think about them now as Arik flicked my clitoris with his tongue, then dipped it inside me.

"He's being stupid. Both of them are. And don't comment on his technique. Mine is all that matters."

Gavin's voice was even fainter.

When I looked back up, both of them were gone, and Arik and I were in my bedroom. I was sprawled on my bed while Arik pressed his mouth against my cunt.

"I'm going to lick you clean," he said gruffly. "Then I'm going to make you wet and we can start all over again."

He slid two fingers inside me, and I cried out, arching my hips up to meet the next thrust, but all he did was lower his mouth, wrapping his lips around my throbbing clit.

"Please," I whimpered. Ready to beg, ready to plead. To promise anything if he'd just give me the release I needed.

"Please what?" Arik looked up, his mouth glistening, wet. As I watched, he licked his lips. "I'll let you pretend to be in charge for a little while, baby. What do you want?"

"I want you to fuck me. I want you to want me."

He crawled up my body, keeping his pressed close to mine. His cock slid against me, but before he gave me what I needed, he stopped, hovering just a breath away as he kissed me. His cock twitched against my hip. "I want you, baby, can't you feel it?"

"You want sex." My eyes fell away from his, and my heart started to ache. "I want..."

I didn't know what I wanted.

Did I?

His hands cupped my face. "I know what you want, my Dena."

He drove inside me then, hard and fast.

"This." He ground his hips against mine, and I whimpered as his cock pulsed inside me. "This..."

But it wasn't.

I cried out against his lips, uncertain how to tell him that I needed more. That I needed something else.

Gripping his shoulders, I arched up under him as he

slammed into me again and again. "Tell me that this is it, Dena... tell me this is what you want..."

He growled the words against my mouth as a climax came rushing up on me.

"Tell me..."

A PHONE RANG, shattering the dream and waking me up.

A dream.

Shit.

Sweat slicked my skin, and everything in me was tensed with the need to come.

And it had been a dream.

The phone rang again, cutting through my still-muddled thoughts. It was my landline and I couldn't figure out why.

Sitting up, I looked around groggily and realized I'd fallen asleep on the sofa, the remains of my sushi sitting on the coffee-table next to the bottle of sake. Dimly, I took a second to be thankful that I wasn't hungover. Then, I grabbed the phone halfway through the third ring, not even thinking to see who was calling.

"Yeah?"

There was a pause, followed by, "Dena?"

I blinked. "Carrie?"

"Ah, yeah. You sound...are you alone?"

"Sadly, yes." The second I said it, I wished I could yank the words back. I ran my hand over my face, trying to wipe away the lingering sleep.

Carrie's chuckle drifted across the line. "Well, I guess that explains that."

"What does it explain?" Weary, aching, and desperate for the climax she interrupted, I stood and gathered up the trash one-handed while clutching the phone with the other hand. She wasn't making any sense and I just wanted her to explain so I could...

"Arik."

I almost dropped the phone and the trash.

"Huh?"

Was this still part of my dream?

"He's here and he looks about as happy as you sound."

For a moment, I thought she meant that Arik had come to her and Gavin's place, but then my brain caught up and I realized she meant that Arik was at the club.

"And you're telling me this why?"

"Because I thought the two of you had made up after Gavin sent you to a room the other night, but now he's here looking like he'd happily rip someone's head off if they look at him cross-eyed. What happened?"

Closing my eyes, I blew out a breath. At least there was a simple way to make her understand. "He's the defense attorney, Carrie."

There was a pause. "He's *a* defense attorney?" she asked delicately.

"Yes. He's also the defense attorney for the defendant whose case I'm assisting on. And I just got moved to second chair." Swallowing, I continued, "Neither of us knew until...the point is, we didn't know. Then we did, but I wasn't going to be co-council. Then Pierce was suspended and now I'm second chair and it's a mess."

Carrie was silent for a moment, and I assumed she was processing the whole mess. "Yeah." Her voice was faint. "Yeah, I guess it is." There was another pause. "Well, I guess that's why you don't have your cell turned on. Trying to avoid him?"

"My boss." Grimacing, I shoved my hair back and squinted at the clock. It was just after ten. I'd slept maybe an hour. "Look,

Carrie, I need to go. I'm exhausted, and I don't want to talk about any of this yet."

"Okay." She hesitated before adding, "You will have to talk about it, though, you know. Soon. You're treading in dangerous waters."

I sighed. "I know."

I hung up and then went through my familiar routine of making sure everything was closed up before I headed to my bedroom. I just wanted to sleep and not think about anything.

I was still lying in bed, staring up at the ceiling nearly an hour later, no rest in sight.

My entire body throbbed, my pussy ached, almost like I could feel him moving inside me, keeping me hovering on the brink without providing any actual relief.

It was too much.

I slid my hands up and down my thighs, closing my eyes. Even that light touch was enough to drive me closer to some edge I could feel deep inside me.

I want you...

The echo of his voice from my dreams wrapped around me. The memory of his hands ghosted over me.

My nipples tightened, rubbing against the thin silk of the camisole I wore. Shifting restlessly, I whimpered when that small movement had my panties moving against my cunt.

Need overwhelmed everything else.

Sliding a hand down my belly, I pushed the tips of my fingers just past the edge of my panties. I let my imagination take over, produce the fantasy I needed.

He hooked his fingers around the lace sidebands of my panties and dragged them down my legs.

As I pushed my fingers inside my wet passage, it was his tongue flicking against me, then entering me.

I'm going to lick you clean...

I moaned as my fingers slid in and out, as the palm of my hand rubbed against my swollen clit.

Tell me you want me...

I did want him.

But there was more. He'd been pushing for something.

I thrust harder, faster, grinding the heel of my hand against my clit.

Now that I was awake, I couldn't deny that there was more to the dream than mere sexual frustration.

And I knew what it was.

I'd avoided it for years, but here, with the worst guy imaginable, I'd gone and fallen for Arik Porter.

The worst man imaginable.

The perfect man.

Bracing my heels against the mattress, I pushed up against my hand and twisted my fingers. A wail ripped out of me, one that had Arik's name echoing off the walls.

As I came back down, I closed my eyes.

I didn't fight the wave of sleep that came over me.

I didn't want to.

Tomorrow would be soon enough to think, soon enough to deal.

TEN
ARIK

Silence wrapped around me as I lay in my bed.

Alone.

I'd given up trying to work at midnight, although realistically, I hadn't gotten anything accomplished most of the evening.

Most of the damn day, really.

Work, productivity, thought...all of it had gone down the drain the moment Bethany had dropped the bomb on me about Dena being moved to second chair.

I told you getting involved was a bad idea.

Dena's voice had been shaking when she said it and even now I could still see the way she'd been struggling against emotion. Pain and anger, and I'd been responsible for most of it.

She'd said it was a bad idea, but I hadn't paid attention, and the second things got dicey, I'd blamed her.

I'd done the one thing a Dom should never do.

I'd put my own wants ahead of her. And I did want her, more than I'd ever wanted anyone before. Even if we hadn't talked about a real relationship, it was always the Dominant's job to take care of their Sub, and I hadn't done that. I'd gotten angry and blamed her simply because it had screwed up what *I* wanted.

Maybe she should've told me as soon as she'd been made second chair, but that didn't excuse my behavior. She was a strong woman, and even though she'd made it clear that she could be a Dominant in her own right, if I wanted the privileges that came with dominating her, I had to accept the responsibilities too.

And I'd fucked up.

It wasn't her fault she ended up with this case. She was a newbie ADA, assigned to a worthless ADA. Although, honestly, for all of Bethany's many faults, it wasn't really her fault Dena and I were on opposite sides of the table. I had no doubt Dena was a great lawyer, which meant she deserved second chair.

Just because I'd spent the weekend thinking about her, instead of digging further into this case, didn't mean I could blame either Dena or Bethany. It'd been hard for me to concentrate, and I could only imagine how difficult it had been for Dena, wondering how to tell me what happened while still trying to catch up. And she'd even managed to find information that actually shot down the motives she was supposed to be supporting.

Bitter humor twisted inside and I recalled what I'd learned from inside sources. They said the prosecution was trying to build a case claiming that Leayna killed her husband because he planned to divorce her and she would lose everything in the process. Except there were no records of him ever having visited or even spoken to a divorce lawyer. I could pick apart their motive without a problem, especially since Dena had made it clear that they didn't have any support for those claims.

I sighed and flung an arm over my eyes, trying to block out everything, including the case...and especially the look Dena had given me before she walked out of the penthouse.

I wasn't going to think about her.

I wasn't going to think about her at all.

Mentally, I focused and began to count down.

Twenty.

Time to let go of all the tension of the day. Deep breath in, out, let it all drift away.

Nineteen.

Loosen the muscles, tighten them, then loosen. From the nape of the neck all the way down.

Eighteen.

Deep breath in, out. Flex the muscles of the lower legs, then release.

Seventeen.

My phone rang.

I jerked upright and grabbed it, hoping against hope that it was Dena.

Staring at the display, at the unknown number showing there, I swore.

So much for not thinking about her.

All the tension I'd managed to wrap under some semblance of control now seemed to be coming back with a vengeance. Swearing, I kicked free of my sheet and punched my fist into the mattress.

This was just a bunch of bullshit, really.

Nothing more.

Ten minutes later, I stood in the shower with a glass of scotch on the shelf beside me, letting myself be wrapped in billows of steam.

If I couldn't talk myself out of thinking about her, I'd do the next best thing. Under normal circumstances, I would've called her, demanding she come over where I'd fuck her out of my mind, but I was starting to think that my usual *normal* might not be possible with her.

And I wasn't sure I wanted it anyway.

Water slid over me, a gentle caress against my skin.

It wasn't even close to as good as having Dena sliding over me, but as I wrapped my hand around my rigid cock, it was pretty clear that my dick didn't care. I was thick, swollen and aching, and what I needed to do was come.

Up, down. Repeat.

Hissing out a breath, I imagined her coming to me through the steam, going to her knees and taking me in her mouth. I stroked my thumb over the head of my penis, imagined it was her tongue. Remembered the heat of her mouth. The suction and pressure.

Inside my head, a hot, X-rated little fantasy played out. Pale in comparison to the real thing, it was enough to keep me going, to make my balls tighten and my body tense.

In the shower, I shifted so that I had my back to the spray, leaning against the wall while I fucked my fist. Water pounded down around me and I panted, teeth peeled back and bared a grimace.

The release that came was just that and only that.

A release.

When I dried off and half-stumbled back to the bed, I had to fight the urge to sigh. It hadn't done much more than take the edge off.

What I needed was Dena.

ELEVEN
DENA

Dreams of Arik chased me all night long.

Waking up feeling like I'd fallen through the looking glass and still hadn't quite found my way out of Wonderland, I gulped down two full cups of coffee even before getting into the shower. I'd grab a third on my way to work.

I wasn't up to verbal sparring today, but I was pretty sure there'd be plenty of it on the plate, so I needed my caffeine.

The dreams...

Even after Carrie had interrupted the first one, more had waited for me.

The second one had been like an acid-laced trip through hell. Not that I'd ever done acid, but a friend had used the description once, and it seemed fitting. It had been all about me and Arik sitting in one of the 'viewing' rooms at Club Privé, while Bethany and her new toy of the week went over reams of paperwork. Naked. There had also been several heads sitting around the room. Just heads. Human heads. Without bodies.

I was positive that paperwork and human heads were important, that they meant something, but damned if I could figure out what.

"If you'd listen to me about how my client was innocent, none of this would be happening." Arik had told me several times in the dream.

"None of *what?*" I muttered out loud now, hours later. "Naked filing?"

Disturbed by all of it, I tried to push the images and voices all out of my head as I showered, but I was only partially successful. By the time I was ready to head out the door, I was so edgy, I actually decided to skip the latte I usually grabbed on the way into the office. If I needed it later, I'd grab one at lunch.

I'd dressed a little more sedately than normal, a concession to my headache and sleepless night. The black pantsuit and vivid pink cami would also be good enough for the club if I lost the jacket, so if I needed to blow off some steam after work, I'd be ready to go. I wasn't going to toss and turn all night like I had last night. Better to dance myself into exhaustion.

Habit had me going straight to my old office. I stopped a few feet away when I remembered, then turned around and trudged back down the hall to where I'd been relocated.

I was halfway there when I collided with Pierce.

Literally.

Crashing into him, I hissed as hot coffee splashed on my hand, and more of it splashed on him.

"Dammit, Dena! Bad enough you're fucking with my career," he snapped, glaring at me. "Do you really need to throw second degree burns on top of it?"

The apology I'd been formulating died on my lips.

"*I'm* fucking with *your* career?" Aware that people were staring at us, I kept my voice low. "I'm not the one who started it, Pierce. All you had to do was speak up."

"And you could have just ignored it and let it go. Nothing would have happened." His eyes darted around, his handsome face an ugly shade of red.

"Wrong." I reigned in my temper. No matter how I felt about him screwing Bethany, she was the one in the position of power. "When you ignore a bully for shit like that, they just do more. They want to see what else they can get away with. How far they can push you." Reaching into the side pocket of my purse, I pulled out a couple of tissues. "Here. For your jacket."

He ignored the offer, continuing to blot at the liquid with an already drenched napkin.

I started to shake my head and step around him, but stopped part-way around. "You know, she's not worth it. She's already trying out her desk with some other guy. Maybe I'm crazy, but I don't think you're a half-bad guy under all of it, Pierce. You could do better. You deserve better."

Before he could say anything else, I headed to my office and shut the door, locking myself in.

———

THE FIRST THREE times I called Bethany, I was snapped at, hung up on, and put on hold for twenty minutes – in that order.

Finally, tired of waiting, I gathered up my notes and the bullet point list I'd made of the reasons why Leayna Mance wasn't the killer. All of which I was almost positive Arik would be presenting in court. We needed to either find ways to refute all of these points, or we needed to find a better suspect. The real suspect.

I just needed to get Bethany to see that.

As soon as I reached Bethany's office, however, I knew things wouldn't be going my way. Her receptionist, Barbara, cut her eyes to the door, then shook her head. Based on the expression on her face, she wasn't merely telling me to sit and wait until Bethany was done with whatever she was doing.

Through the partially open door, I could hear Bethany talking. As there wasn't anybody responding to her curt questions, I had to assume she was on the phone.

I settled myself in one of the chairs and gave Barbara a little smile. In her fifties, she once told me she was counting down the months to retirement. I was pretty sure she only had eight months left. I couldn't imagine having to work eight months directly under Bethany. At least now I could escape to my office most of the time.

There was a heavy smashing sound and Barbara and I shared a grimace before Bethany appeared in the doorway. Her glare flew past me to lock on her receptionist. "Find out who in the *fuck* is handling the docket this afternoon. I want a name. They're going to be very sorry they fucked with me." She drew in another breath and then stopped, her gaze drifting back toward me. "Did we have something scheduled?" she asked, her voice icy.

"No." I managed a polite smile. "I can always set up a time for later, but I had a few things about the Mance case that I needed to discuss with you, and I wasn't having much luck calling you earlier."

"This was why I wanted Lawton on the case," she said, turning on her heel and stalking into her office. "He seems perfectly capable of working independently."

Since she hadn't closed the door, I assumed that meant I was to follow.

"As it seems he's back from his suspension, perhaps you'd prefer him to resume being second chair." I kept my voice neutral.

"No," she snapped. "The back and forth is slowing things down, and it won't look good when we finally get to move to court. Speaking of which..." She took up position behind the desk and spread her hands wide on the surface before giving me a hard look. "You had something to discuss. Let's hear it."

Placing my file down on the desk, I flipped it open.

"Nothing about this case adds up," I said bluntly. She wouldn't like it, but at least she wouldn't throw me out before I had my say. "Mrs. Mance is being painted as a woman scorned, murdering her husband for planning to divorce her, and leaving her with nothing. Except no one can find any record of him even speaking with a divorce lawyer."

"All he had to do was say it, and it set her off." Bethany crossed her arms over her chest.

"But there's no proof," I continued. "And according to their pre-nup, if he filed for divorce for anything other than infidelity, he had to pay her half."

"Just because we haven't found proof of an affair doesn't mean it didn't happen."

I took a slow breath. "We have no motive, and none of the forensics supports her being the killer."

"She was in the building," Bethany snapped. "She had his blood on her."

"But not as much as she would have if she'd killed him. The medical examiner said that the killer would've been covered from head-to-toe. The pictures of Ms. Mance after the fact show blood on her shirt and her hands, nowhere else."

"Dammit, Dena! Are you a prosecutor or her bleeding heart defense attorney?"

"I'm a lawyer, same as you. And things don't add up. We might be prosecuting the wrong person."

Bethany snorted, the sound thick with scorn. "Oh, honey. You need to grow up." She gestured toward the file as if she didn't even want to touch it. "Put that away. This is about getting a conviction."

I squared my shoulders and asked the question I hadn't wanted to ask. "And if an innocent person goes to jail?"

An unladylike noise came from her throat. "Don't be so naïve, Dena. Nobody's innocent."

Nobody's innocent.

There was nothing Bethany could have said that would've pissed me off quite as much as those two simple words.

It wasn't just the opposite of people who thought everyone was innocent. Thinking that nobody was innocent, in Bethany's mind, seemed to be a free pass to charge anyone with any crime, whether they did it or not, simply because they must be guilty of something.

I knew that, more and more, the belief of innocent until proven guilty was being put through the ringer, especially by the media. It annoyed me, but it wasn't the same.

Bethany made a mockery of everything I'd chosen to believe in, everything I wanted to believe in. She preferred to ignore all the evidence pointing to the possibility that her suspect might be innocent. She just wanted to put someone away, get a win. Justice didn't matter to her.

I still believed in justice, and I'd do what I needed to make sure that it was served.

Even if that meant going over Bethany's head with any evidence I found.

At least it seemed like I'd have plenty of time to work. Pierce was going out of his way to avoid me. Since he wasn't working on anything connected to the Mance case now, it was easy to stay away from him without actually looking like I was avoiding him. And, of course, Bethany was tied up in court. If the courthouse grapevine was anywhere near accurate, she'd nailed somebody's ass to a wall on the stand just the other day.

Between now and Monday morning, I probably didn't have to worry much about Bethany appearing at my shoulder or calling me. Her current case would probably be going to closing arguments tomorrow and handed off to the jury over the weekend.

Come Monday, though, Bethany would be on my ass again. More importantly, she'd be looking for a way to lock Leayna Mance up for a murder I was becoming more and more certain she hadn't committed.

If she's innocent, you just need to find a way to prove it, I told myself. Regardless of what Bethany said, there was more to my job as a prosecutor then putting people in prison. Everybody lost when an innocent person was found guilty.

I kept that in mind as I stayed closeted away from the world, feeling more and more isolated as Thursday wore on. Except for a text from Carrie, I didn't speak to anybody outside a few people to request evidence.

Well, and the barista on the corner.

I really wouldn't have minded a call, say from somebody like Arik.

But the phone stayed stubbornly silent.

"YOU'RE LOOKING in the wrong place."

Arik slid his hands up my torso. His mouth grazed mine

before he caught my wrists and guided them behind my back. "You should have told me about getting second chair. You didn't. Now I'm going to punish you."

The shiver that slid through me was delicious. I shouldn't have felt so excited. I was still mad at him, wasn't I? And I had a right to be. Didn't I?

Making myself look at him, I said, "I was going to tell you. I just needed time to think about what it meant."

"You could have thought about it and told me. We could've talked about it. If we're going to have a relationship, we don't hide things. We talk." He tugged me closer, tucking me up against him so that his cock was pressed against my ass. "So...do we have a relationship?"

"Yes." I whimpered as I said it, loving the way it twisted something inside me. Something stroked me between my thighs, dragging a moan from my lips. "Are you...how are you going to punish me, Arik?"

He laughed, the sound low and husky.

"You know you deserve to be punished, don't you?"

Face flushed and hot, I nodded. "Yes."

"Good."

He stroked a hand down my hair and stepped away. I strained to see him and that was when I realized I was tied to a chair. My office chair. And I was naked.

He passed in front of me, tapping a crop against his thigh. I licked my lips and Arik wagged a finger at me. "Don't go getting impatient, Dena. This is the reward. Not the punishment. You only get the reward if you solve the puzzle."

"What puzzle?"

He gestured toward my desk.

"That's the punishment. You have to solve the puzzle."

Confused, I shook my head. "That's not how this works. Arik, untie me."

"No. You have to solve the puzzle. Look again."

I looked and this time, I saw something else. The courthouse. In miniature. Like a dollhouse.

I tried to stand up and realized I could.

I was dressed again, and Arik was gone. I wasn't worried about that though. I was focused on the puzzle. Moving forward, I stared down into the courthouse. The roof was gone and I could see a miniature me standing outside Bethany's office. She was in there, with that guy.

"Solve the puzzle."

I jumped at the sound of Arik's voice.

He was behind me and I almost yelped.

He grinned at me, his teeth flashing white. "Jumpy, Dena. You should get more sleep. You wouldn't be so nervous. Who is he, Dena?" He pointed at Bethany and her...friend.

"I don't know!"

"That's the puzzle." Arik went back to staring at the miniature of the man I'd seen with Bethany. "Solve it and you can have your reward."

The miniature man and Bethany weren't having sex now. The man was going through the papers on Bethany's desk and Bethany...I swallowed when I realized she was on the floor with a bright red dot in the middle of her forehead.

"What happens if I don't solve it, Arik?" I didn't look at him as I asked the question.

He hugged me against him. "You have to, Dena."

I JERKED AWAKE, my temples throbbing. That hadn't been the best dream I'd ever had. If anything, it just made things worse. Then I looked down at my desk and sighed as I remembered why I'd closed my eyes for just a minute.

"This doesn't make sense."

Rubbing my temples, I went over the figures again.

I didn't know why I was even bothering, because I'd already done the calculations a good four times, and had come up with the same result.

It wasn't my math that was wrong.

As much as I hated finances, over the past few years, I'd become depressingly good at eyeballing things and seeing where the discrepancies were, where the lies hid. Too many of my former clients had spouses who tried hiding money to avoid claiming the assets. Then there'd been the ones who tried hiding an affair or some sort of crime.

If there was one thing I'd learned from years as a divorce lawyer, it was that numbers talked.

And these numbers were telling one hell of a story.

Mr. Mance had spent more money than he'd made, and his corporation had been in trouble. He'd tried to get loans over the past year, probably trying to shore things up, but he'd been turned down.

"Banks know a bad bet." Blowing out a hard breath, I leaned back and studied the sheets filled with my scrawling notes.

The data for the business had all looked pretty much the same for three years running, right up until six months into this past year. Then, things had turned around. A sudden influx of money. I would've assumed a loan, but there was no sign anybody legit had paid anything out. However, he'd suddenly been able to do exactly what needed to be done, shored up some of the areas that were bleeding money, cut some of them off entirely. He'd managed to salvage his company.

I just had no idea how he'd done it.

"Where did he get the money?" I ran my finger down the column more slowly.

Shit.

There it was.

Fifty thousand.

In cash.

My heart thudded loudly in the silence.

Coincidence.

Had to be.

But...

I ran my hands over my face. The police had searched the apartment of my dead police informant slash possible witness.

And they'd found a bag of fifty thousand dollars in cash.

Officer Dunne had told me that the rumor around the station was that the guy had been involved in organized crime. I'd originally thought that the man had been Mance's lover, though that hadn't been an angle I would've brought up to Bethany unless I had proof. Now, however, I was thinking that might not have been true. Or, at least not the whole truth.

Organized crime. Large amounts of cash found. Equal deposits of cash. Secret meetings at strip clubs.

What the hell had Mance gotten himself into?

THIRTEEN

I'd had worse weeks.

Really, aside from one personal matter, things hadn't completely sucked. It was just that the one *personal matter* had colored everything else I'd done.

"Personal matter," I muttered, climbing out of my car and tossing my keys to the valet outside the building. I paid a small fortune just to keep a car in the city, but I was too used to having my own transportation. The few times I'd tried car services and taxis, it'd been all I could do not to backseat drive.

"Sir?"

I looked over and saw the valet's puzzled expression and realized I'd been grumbling out loud. "Sorry. Just talking to myself."

"Of course." He nodded as if that was perfectly normal.

Then again, I could've told him that I was talking to an elephant in a pink tutu, and he wouldn't have blinked. When you had money, you were allowed more than a few eccentricities. People excused all sorts of shit when dollar signs got involved.

Which was why I didn't really let anyone know that I had

money. I liked people taking me at face value, for who they thought I was or wasn't, just based on how I acted.

Like with Dena. I'd acted like an asshole, and now she was making it pretty damn clear that she wasn't impressed.

What in the hell had I been thinking?

As I headed into the high rise, I debated on whether or not to call her. She'd said she needed space, time to figure things out. I'd given her that. A few days, at least. But if she didn't have an idea about whether or not she was going to forgive me by now, then I'd like to know when she thought she might be ready to talk to me.

Besides, I should apologize, right? I'd been a tool.

In front of the elevator bay, I glared at the numbers as if they were responsible for how things were going between Dena and me. I might have continued to do that if somebody hadn't delicately cleared her throat. Jerking myself out of the brooding haze, I looked up just in time to see a thin blonde dressed in yoga gear lean over and punch a button.

She gave me a cautious look, one of those speculative looks that I might've acted on a couple of months ago.

Instead of initiating a conversation or even smiling, I just nodded and punched in my own floor. We rose in silence, and she got off first. When I reached my floor, however, instead of going to my apartment, I headed out to the rooftop to think.

Somebody was up there smoking. That went against the tenant's rental agreement, but as long as they kept the smoke on that side of the building where the wind could grab it, I didn't care. Hands braced on the railing, I stared out over the sprawling Manhattan skyline.

Part of me was homesick. Not for Chicago, exactly, but for the friends and family I had there. I might've grown up with money, but my family had never really seen themselves as rich. We worked hard for our money, got our hands dirty alongside our employees. There'd been no hard feelings when I'd gone into law instead of business. I'd been grateful for it, just as I'd always been grateful that my parents hadn't cared if my friends were rich, poor or in-between. Some had moved away after high school, some after college, but there'd always been someone I could call to go out and have a drink with when I needed one.

And I sure as hell needed one right now. Both a listening ear, and a drink.

This whole case was rubbing me the wrong way and not just because of Dena. *That* was pissing me off, but that wasn't the main thing nagging at me.

The case...I didn't like anything about it.

I'd talked to the cops who'd handled the investigation and any number of steps had been missed. The autopsy had pointed at somebody other than Leayna, but no one had made much noise about that. She was tall, but still not tall enough to have created the right angle for the wounds. And then there had been her clothes. She hadn't had enough blood on her face or her clothes. I knew Bethany would argue that Leayna had changed into something else before calling me and the cops, but there wasn't any forensics to support that either.

I pointed all of this out just a day ago when I managed to get a judge to talk to me about the case. He'd nodded and smiled, and then told me to present my findings in court. When I said I planned to file for a dismissal, he flat-out told me that he wouldn't rule for that. In his mind, if a grand jury had seen fit to indict, then there should be a trial.

So, unless there was a plea deal – or the real killer came forward – we were going to court. Possibly as early as next week, although I'd already put things in motion to stop that from happening. Bethany seemed determined to get through this as quickly as possible, and that made me that much more determined to slow it down, let other evidence have time to come to light.

Thunder rumbled overhead, and I lifted my gaze, staring up at the clouds gathering overhead. A fat raindrop fell, hitting me right between the eyes. Somewhere off to the east, lightning cracked down and the smell of ozone tinged the air.

"Can't even get a brood-on going with this case," I scowled. Even Mother Nature was against me.

Shoving away from the railing, I turned. I paused, though, when I saw the guy with the cigarette still there. Leaning against the railing, his gaze was fixed in my direction.

I had the weirdest feeling he'd been staring at me.

And that wasn't creepy at all.

His face was too far away for me to make out details, but as rain began to beat down on the rooftop, he didn't move. The cherry-red tip of his cigarette went out, but he stayed there, half-hidden in the shadows, and I knew I was right. He was watching me.

Shit.

Starting toward the door, I kept my steps slow and even, my body balanced so I could fight if necessary. I'd never been mugged, and I had no intention to experience it any time soon.

But he never moved.

Once I was inside, I debated on calling building security, but if the guy had just been staring off into space or even watching me because he was trying to figure out if he knew me, I didn't want him to get in trouble. Besides, I was determined not to be *that* tenant who acted like everything was all about them.

I shook my head as I headed for the stairwell, ready to get inside my apartment now. Take a hot shower, have a scotch. Call Dena.

I almost reconsidered that last thought, but I really didn't want to.

I needed to talk to her. I couldn't think clearly when it came to her, and I was just realizing that when things weren't right between us, it was even worse. I needed to call her and make things right, then focus on the case so I could get through it.

Once that was done, I could focus on Dena. I'd figure out a way to make things work, even if she was with the DA's office. There were ways. I just had to find them.

Mind made up, I swung around the landing for the third and last flight of stairs. In the natural pause between my steps, I heard a faint squeak. The same squeak I'd heard when I opened the rooftop door a few minutes ago.

Shit.

I didn't know why that guy had been looking at me, but I didn't want to be alone in a stairwell with him.

I wasn't an idiot.

I pulled out my keys and hurried down the last few stairs. I hadn't been in New York long enough to have any former clients or family members of former clients pissed at me. And I seriously doubted anyone from Chicago would've followed me. Most of my stuff had been white-collar crimes.

Then I remembered the threats Leayna had gotten.

Shit.

I pushed inside, thinking only about getting the door closed behind me.

If I'd taken a moment, I might have noticed a few things.

Like the fact that all of the lights were off even though I always left the entryway light on.

I might have noticed that the alarm wasn't beeping its annoying little reminder to disarm it.

I might have noticed the shadow in the corner *before* he spoke.

"It would seem my associate was both right and wrong."

At the sound of the voice, I tensed, but didn't run. I reached over and turned on the lights.

A man sat in a chair, a gun pointed square at my chest.

I didn't try to fight the panic that automatically came when I saw the gun. It was a human response. All I needed to do was hide it. Voice calm, I said, "I didn't realize I had an after-hours meeting scheduled tonight."

"You're a cool one." He jabbed the revolver at me, grinning wide enough to show a gold-capped tooth on the bottom. "Drop the phone."

I glanced down at it, almost negligently and shrugged before tossing it down.

He didn't say anything about the keys, and I wondered if he'd noticed them. I held them cupped loosely in my hand which meant it was possible he hadn't seen them, although how he thought I'd gotten in, I didn't know. Not really my problem if he didn't notice them. I was more interested in what was going to happen next.

He held the gun like a man who knew how to use it, and I suspected he was a man who didn't *care* if he had to use it or not. I didn't think he planned on killing me tonight, but I also didn't think he would care if his plans were changed. It wouldn't matter to him if I lived or died. That much was clear.

"Have a seat," he said, a faint smile curving his lips. "We should talk."

There was a faint accent to his words, very faint. It was like he'd grown up speaking another language, but had long since switched to English. I couldn't quite place it though.

"If we're talking, mind if I get a drink?" I asked as I took a step forward. "I was planning on doing that as soon as I got home anyway."

"Sit. I'll get." The words grew shorter, more tense and the accent was a bit more pronounced. "I'll have drink, too."

Slavic, I thought. Maybe...

Fuck. Everything came together all at once.

Leayna's husband had connections to the mafia, the *Russian* mafia. And now I had an accented man with a gun in my living room. Probably a hitman.

Deciding it wasn't wise to argue with him, I settled in a seat, still gripping my keys, and watched as he circled around the room toward the wet bar I'd set up in the corner. It was fully stocked already. He studied everything with a faint smile before cocking his head at me. I never once got the impression he was distracted. He was making a show of letting me think he was distracted by the bar service. I wasn't that stupid, though. I'd wait to make my move.

"At least you have good vodka," he said.

"Well, you never know when you'll have your friendly local Russian mafia hitman stop by for a drink." I shrugged as I said it, although I was hoping those wouldn't be the last words I said.

He flashed me a wide smile. "Yes. I am the friendly one. If they had sent Olaf, he would have already just beaten the information out of you and cut your throat. I prefer...less messy tactics. We are more civilized these days."

"So you don't plan on cutting my throat?" I wasn't buying it.

"Only if I have to." He picked up a bottle and studied it. "You like this one?"

He'd picked up the Macallan.

"Yes."

He opened it, sniffed. "Not bad. I shall try this instead of vodka. We'll share a drink, talk."

Wonderful.

As he splashed the expensive scotch into two highballs, I carefully lowered the keys so they were in the seat next to my thigh, out of sight. I wasn't considering using them as a weapon, not unless they were a last resort. I wanted to keep them with me because the key fob for the panic alarm was on it. He'd disarmed my system. Not just disarmed it, but deactivated it entirely. I could see the control panel was open, wires sticking out. But hopefully the panic button on the key fob would still work.

Once I pushed it, cops would be here in maybe ten minutes.

If it worked.

If it didn't...well, I would just have to see what Mr. Civilized wanted, and maybe just how good I was at extricating myself from sticky situations.

"You look like a man thinking serious thoughts."

I blinked everything back into focus as he came around the wet bar, holding both of the glasses in one hand. He paused by the chair where he'd been sitting, and after a deliberate look at me, put the gun down on the arm of the chair so he could relieve himself of one of the scotches. I didn't do anything. He was too far away, and I wasn't about to delude myself into thinking I could get to him quicker than he could pick up that gun and kill me. Or maybe shoot out my kneecaps so he could still question me.

"You are a cool one," he murmured again as he picked up the gun before coming over to offer me my drink.

I accepted the scotch with a steady hand and tossed back half of it. Apparently, he had an iron liver because he'd filled the highball well over halfway. I drained half of it in that first swallow.

He chuckled as he backed away and then settled back down in the chair across from me. "Now, we can talk."

"Like civilized men."

"Exactly." He took his scotch and lifted it in my direction in a salute.

I saluted him in similar fashion, and held still as he took a slow, savoring sip.

"It is good," he said approvingly. "I cannot do business with a man who doesn't have decent taste in alcohol." He took another sip and then put the glass down. "We need to discuss your client."

"I can't discuss my clients."

He grinned. "Client confidentiality. You will use that when I have this pointed at you?"

Dropping my gaze to the gun, I swallowed. I'd never thought I might have to consider client confidentiality over my own life, but I'd taken an oath.

"It is a good thing they sent me instead of Olaf," he murmured.

I looked away from the gun to meet his eyes. He was nodding to himself as if he'd reached some deep, meaningful conclusion.

"He would have decided to beat you on principle the first time you showed any sign of having a spine. Me, I appreciate a man with courage. But it might end up getting you killed, Mr. Porter."

Yeah, that's about what I expected.

He leaned forward and pinned me with cold, hard eyes. His accent thickened. "Don't discuss the case. I do not give a flying fuck. Here is what we need to discuss. Your client needs to plead out. We already told her this and she was ready to do it. You must have talked her out of it. Change her mind again. She will plead out, plead guilty to murder, manslaughter, whatever the fuck. She pleads out."

I stared at him, working at keeping the blank expression that usually came so easily to me.

"Do you understand what I'm telling you?"

That was easy enough to answer. "I understand what you're saying."

His lids flickered. I had a feeling he wasn't fooled by my response into thinking I was agreeing to do what he said.

"Her husband had something that belonged to my employer. And because the son of a bitch decided to play hardball, he's dead. We told him what would happen. He didn't believe us. Now she gets to suffer the consequences."

My mind had been piecing everything together and with this, the rest came together. "Are you telling me that Leayna has been caught up in this solely because her husband was an asshole?"

"She married the asshole. She stayed with him." He shrugged, looking unperturbed. Scraping his short nails down the stubble on his cheek, he said, "You know, I have a good relationship with the boss. I could...well, *perhaps* I could suggest he leave her alone if she'll give him what her husband tried to cheat him out of. He tried to find it already, but it wasn't there."

The final piece. "The break-in."

His eyes gleamed. "She is lucky she wasn't there. Olaf had been given permission to do whatever was needed."

Olaf could get fucked.

"Would you like to know what my boss is looking for?" he asked softly, leaning forward.

Solve the puzzle.

My mind kept going back to those words Arik had spoken during my little nap. *Solve the puzzle.* Personally, I would've preferred to linger on that crop and all of the wonderful things I was sure my imagination would've come up with, but first things first.

The puzzle of Bethany and her desktop lover.

It wasn't surprising that she'd already found somebody to take Pierce's place. Although, it was highly possible that Pierce had never really had a place. Not that he'd known that. There'd been real surprise in his eyes when I'd mentioned the other guy. No denying that.

Solve the puzzle, Arik's voice whispered again.

Not his voice, really. My subconscious.

"The puzzle of *what?*"

I knew it had something to do with Bethany and the guy, but what about them? Or was it more him than them?

"The guy," I mumbled, answering my own question.

The swaying of the subway came to a stop. Automatically, I looked up to make sure I hadn't missed my exit. That was when

I realized a couple of people were watching me. The second I looked up, though, they busied themselves with something else, anything else, even if it was just to study their own fingernails.

Apparently, I'd been musing my problems out loud. Looking out my window, I rolled my eyes and ignored the other people. It was the New York subway, for crying out loud. All sorts of people talked to themselves on the subway. Granted, not too many of them were dressed in a chic little suit and carrying a briefcase that cost a few hundred dollars, but seriously. If you couldn't be eccentric on the New York City subway, where could you be eccentric?

As the train started to pull ahead, I took note of where we were. One stop from where I needed to get off. Gathering my things, I stood up and moved closer to the exit.

Once through the doors and onto the platform, I went through the tangle of people, and started for the surface, my mind already back on Bethany and her man. More specifically, on him. I'd seen him somewhere before. Where did I know him from?

The jangling of my phone interrupted my reverie, and I came to a halt in front of a big, plate glass window as I stopped to tug my phone free. Eyes on the TV on the other side of the window, I answered the phone without looking to see who was calling. It was Carrie's new ringtone.

I didn't get it out in time to keep Carrie's call from rolling over to voicemail. Sighing, I pulled up my call log and hit her number, eyes still on the daily news that the electronics chain had blasting across the screen.

I rolled my eyes at some of the headlines, fought a pang at one of them. Typical day in the Big Apple. A cop was in trouble in this precinct, while in another, one had taken down some career criminal who never should have been released from prison to begin with.

There was another terrorist threat, and the mayor was assuring New Yorkers and our numerous visitors to continue life as always. We'd mourn, we'd get pissed and we'd carry on.

Carrie came on the line just as a prominent NYPD lieutenant's face came on the screen. The text down at the bottom of the screen read:

Second alleged NYPD snitch found murdered, dismembered in dumpster in Harlem precinct.

"HEY, STRANGER," Carrie said. "You never write. You never call…"

"You too good to talk to voice mail now that you're engaged to a seriously hot and rich man?" I asked distractedly, my head cocked as I stared at the TV. Every single thought in my head seemed to stutter to a stop.

Solve the puzzle.

The words seemed to echo in my head now, growing louder and louder and louder.

"And when was the last time we talked?" she demanded.

"Over the weekend. I texted two days ago." Moving closer, I squinted my eyes, although that wouldn't make it any easier to hear what was going on. The sound was probably muted. The captions were rolling, but they were patchy. Better than nothing. Reading them, I managed to catch up enough to have an idea of what was going on.

"Yeah, yeah. So what?" Carrie didn't sound impressed. "Hey, we haven't talked, seriously, in forever. If you're not doing anything, why don't you come down to the club?"

"Can't." My eyes raced back and forth over the captions. Shifting the weight of my briefcase and purse, mind whirling, I tried to keep up with Carrie and with what I was reading. This was it. *This* was the puzzle. "I'm too distracted. The case, Carrie. Something big just came up."

She said something, but I didn't really process it. Everything inside me seemed to be on edge, processing what I'd just figured out.

The puzzle.

I was pretty sure I was getting close to figuring out the puzzle.

I didn't realize I'd spoken out loud until Carrie asked, "What puzzle? Dena, are you okay?"

"No. Yeah." I shook my head, trying to clear it. "Have you seen today's news?"

"Same old crazy shit for New York."

"Yeah." I shifted my weight from one foot to the other. "The guy they think was a snitch. He's dead. There was another one, too. Two snitches, dead. I wonder if he was connected to the mafia."

Carrie groaned. "The mafia. Hell, Dena. You know how trite that is? The mafia and New York. People still think they might run afoul of the mafia if they simply come to New York. I've lived here all my life, and I've never so much as met a single Mafioso type."

"That's because the Italian mafia isn't what it used to be. People just think it is. This..." I blew out a breath, barely hearing what I was saying. "The Russian mafia, the Mexican cartels? Those are the big problems now."

Arik's voice vibrated inside my head again, and now, as if they were in front of me, I could see Bethany and her guy again. Then she faded out, like a washed out, old photograph and all I could see was him.

The guy.

He was in stark, clear color. Those harsh, cut cheek-bones, high, arched eyebrows and dark eyes. Eyes that were almost black. He was handsome, in a cold, brutal way.

Cold.

Brutal.

Yeah, that summed it up.

I'd thought that the first time I'd seen him, and suddenly realized that it hadn't been with Bethany a few days ago.

"Oh, *shit*," I whispered as it slammed into me.

I knew his face alright. His face, yes. But not him.

I'd never seen him in person before that night, but I'd known that face all the same.

"Okay," Carrie said, her voice holding a note of finality. "That's it. You're going to tell me what's going on."

"I can't." Clearing my throat, I turned away from the news cast. A sense of foreboding washed over me, and I had to fight to keep from sending furtive glances all over the place.

"You damn well better," she retorted. "You're starting to freak me out."

"I'm fine." I'm pretty sure I even sounded like I believed it. Which was good. I didn't need carry or Gavin to come rushing out looking for me. Not now that I finally figured it out. Not now that I finally solved the damn puzzle.

The last thing I needed to do was put my friends in the same danger I was pretty sure I was putting myself in if I kept digging into Leayna Mance's case.

"I just figured out something pretty important to my case, Carrie. I can't talk about it, though. And I kind of need to go. It's important."

Talk about the understatement of the year.

She huffed out a sigh. "Fine. I wish I didn't understand that *I can't* so well, but a lawyer's oath doesn't change, no matter what type of law we practice. Call me when you can. And whatever it is, kick its ass, okay?"

"Yeah." I managed a weak smile as I disconnected and stood there, staring at absolutely nothing.

What in the hell was I supposed to do now?

My skin was crawling as I stood out there on the street. It had nothing to do with the stories I'd seen on the news, though, and all to do with the things that I'd finally managed to put together.

My potential witness, the police informant. He'd been Russian. And he'd been connected to Leayna Mance's husband.

Oh shit.

The Russian mafia.

Arik had been so convinced his client was innocent. *So* convinced that there was something else going on. He was right, dammit.

I'd had more than a few reservations of my own, all of it because things just didn't add up and Bethany had refused to listen to me. That had rubbed me wrong, although now even that made a twisted sort of sense.

Swallowing hard, I made myself take one step, then another. It wasn't likely that I had people following me, not really. But if I did, it would be best if I acted normal, right?

That guy in Bethany's office. He was connected to the mafia. Connected in the worst possible way. He was also wanted. Not just by the NYPD, but by the FBI and probably several other law enforcement agencies. Wanted on the national, and possibly the international, level.

He was a known hit man for the Russian mafia.

And my *boss*, an assistant district attorney for Manhattan, had been fucking him.

Shit.

"Talk about sleeping with the enemy."

After five minutes of being completely shocked into silence, I finally managed to come up with something to say.

My boss – the Manhattan assistant district attorney who was supposed to be training me, teaching me the ropes, making sure I didn't screw up or get in trouble – was sleeping with a man suspected of being a hitman from the Russian mafia. This wasn't just a rumor either. Or something I merely suspected. I'd actually seen Bethany McDermott bent over her desk, the strange man I just identified pounding into her from behind.

A chill raced down my spine, and despite the warmth that came with the press of bodies around me, I felt cold.

I could have bundled up in front of a fire and still been cold.

It didn't help that my clothes were damp. I'd started walking almost automatically after hanging up on Carrie, ending up half-soaked before I even realized it. I managed to take refuge in the nearest coffee shop, along with what felt like half of New York City, but even the smell of coffee hadn't been able to get my mind off of what I'd seen.

But the rain had stopped a few minutes ago, and now I was

walking along the street, taking my time as I made my way home.

I had to...

I stopped in the middle of the sidewalk – a cardinal sin in New York City.

Somebody crashed into me, knocking me out of my daze, and I offered a distracted apology as I moved over to the side and stared out into the crowd. I couldn't keep from looking around me, my eyes bouncing from one face to the next. I didn't know what I was looking for, or maybe hoping to find, but there was something.

I was looking for something.

Somebody.

An attack maybe. I felt like I was caught in a spotlight, that somebody was going to swoop down and pull a gun on me, shoot me for what I'd seen.

I knew something now, didn't I? Did that make me a risk? Someone who needed to be eliminated? Was that how it worked?

"You're being paranoid," I muttered.

But even as that thought faded from my mind, I realized something crucial. I couldn't go back to the office on Monday. What was I going to do? Confront Bethany? No way in hell. But then who could I talk to? I didn't know anybody at the DA's office I trusted well enough for something this potentially deadly. For all I knew, there were half a dozen dirty ADA's.

To be honest, outside of Carrie, Krissy, and Leslie, the list of people I'd trust with this information was decidedly short. And I wasn't going to put any of my friends in danger. They might claim to be able to take care of themselves, and maybe they could, but I sure as hell wasn't going to put that to the test. Maybe Gavin or DeVon, if he'd been on this side of the country. But maybe not even them. They were Alpha Male with a capital *A*. They would've called the cops and not let me out of their sight.

A face flickered through my mind and I went rigid.

Arik.

I could go to Arik.

That would probably be the stupidest thing to do, but the moment the thought crossed my mind, the muscles in my shoulders started to relax, and I managed to take my first easy breath since I'd seen Bethany in her compromising position. My nerves were stretched so taut that I felt like even the slightest touch would break me. Talking to Arik might help. Even if he was too new in the city to have a lot of contacts, maybe he'd have at least a general idea of where to start.

"Grasping at straws." Shaking my head at myself, I moved to the edge of the curb and held up a hand, waiting for a cab.

I probably *was* grasping at straws, but one thing was certain – between Arik and a stranger at the DA's office, Arik was the safest option. Talking to him might be a bit unethical, but it wasn't like I was planning on discussing the case. And I knew, with him, I didn't have to worry about him telling the wrong person, resulting in me getting acquainted with the business end of something sharp and shiny.

I tried calling his number, but no one answered. I wasn't sure if that meant he was busy or if he was just ignoring me. Either one was a possibility, I supposed. I left a brief voicemail, asking him to call me back, but not giving any details. This wasn't the sort of thing I wanted a recording of.

Him not answering, however, meant I'd have to find him and hope he'd agree to talk to me. I didn't know exactly where the two of us stood at the moment, but I was fairly confident it wasn't bad enough that he'd turn me away without hearing what I had to say.

I didn't know the exact address of the place where Arik had

taken me earlier this week, and I didn't even know if he was living there or somewhere else while it was being finished, but it was a place to start. My only other options were to go to his office and hope he'd worked late, or find out if there was any way Officer Dunne could get the information. Most defense attorneys, even ones who'd been born and raised in New York, didn't have their home addresses available to the public.

I was going to take my chances with the first option before I did anything else. I was second chair on a case that Arik was trying. Showing up at his office would probably be a bad idea. The less people who knew that the two of us were acquainted outside of the courtroom, the better. But, if I had to, I'd go there.

I needed to talk to someone, and he was my best option.

Even if I wasn't entirely sure how I felt about him at the moment.

An idea occurred to me as I was waiting for a cab to finally notice my out-stretched hand, and I felt dumb for having not thought of it first. I'd been so focused on seeing him, I hadn't considered calling first. At least that way, I'd know where he was.

When I couldn't reach him on his cell, I tapped my screen to call his office. A woman answered on the second ring. "Sheldon, Simon and Sharpe. How can I help you?"

"Good evening." I worked to make my voice as business-like as possible. "I'm with the DA's office and I need to speak to Mr. Arik Porter."

"He's not here right now," the woman replied. "Can I take a message?"

"No," I said quickly. Then, before I could stop myself, I asked, "Is he at home?"

There was a momentary pause, then the woman's voice got decidedly cooler. "I'm sorry. I can't give out personal information."

"Of course," I said. "I'll call back tomorrow."

When I ended the call, I closed my eyes for a moment. That had been stupid, asking if he was at home. For all that woman knew, I was some psycho former client. Just because I said I was from the DA's office didn't mean I actually was.

I opened my eyes and told myself that it didn't matter. I'd at least narrowed down the possibilities of where he was. I supposed it was possible that he'd gone out, but I wouldn't bother trying to figure any of that out until I found out if he was home or not.

A cab finally pulled up to the curb and I got inside. I was going to go broke on cab fare the way things were going lately. I gave the address and settled back into the seat. At this time in the evening, it would take a while to get there.

As we inched forward, my phone started to ring. I wasn't able to get it out of my purse before it stopped ringing, but I looked at the screen anyway. I hoped it was Arik, that he'd somehow sensed how much I needed to talk to him and had gotten back to me right away. It was silly, I knew, because we weren't like that, and even if we were, things like that were romanticized. Arik and I were logical people. We thought things through.

I frowned when the words *unknown caller* popped up on my screen. Whoever it was, it looked like they'd left a voicemail at least. I glanced up and saw that we'd only gone a couple blocks. At this rate, I might've been able to walk there faster.

I called the voicemail, thankful that I had a fairly taciturn cab driver. There was a long buzz of dead air before I heard...something. My frown deepened as I strained to listen.

There was a series of muttering voices, mumbles more than anything else. I was about ready to lower the phone and delete it when something sharp and ear-piercing came through the receiver.

A scream that cut off abruptly when the call ended.

I almost dropped my phone.

"What was the street number again, miss?"

Jerking my head up, I looked at the cab driver. Shaken, but fighting not to show it, I told him. Then I clamped my mouth shut before I could ask him to hurry the hell up. Suddenly, I needed to see Arik, and it wasn't because I was worried about me anymore.

SIXTEEN
ARIK

My cell phone rang for the second time in a space of ten minutes. Not that I could answer it this time any more than the last. With it being face-down, I couldn't even see if it was the same person calling.

It lay on the plush, steel gray carpet of my entry way, some fifteen feet away from me...and from my friendly neighborhood hitman. He flicked a look at it before shifting his attention back to me and smiling.

I had to give him credit. If he'd been a man I had to defend, it would've been a piece of cake to coach him. He was actually quite polite, charming even. He'd be the kind of man who'd be cool-headed on the stand when questioned about a murder, but not make the jury think he was being cold.

Then he could go out and put a bullet in someone's head without blinking an eye.

A good thing in a defendant. Not such a good thing when the man had a gun pointed in my direction.

"The second time. You are quite popular. Are you expecting to speak with someone tonight?" His accent was Russian. Maybe one of the surrounding countries. I couldn't quite distinguish it, especially since it was fairly faint. He'd been in this country for a while.

Lifting one shoulder, I said, "I'm a lawyer. I'm always expecting calls. Alleged criminals don't always keep usual work hours."

It was both the honest truth and the best non-answer I could come up with. I also thought it couldn't hurt to throw a little humor into the mix.

He looked amused, so I supposed that was a good thing. A happy hit-man was less likely to kill me, right?

When the phone went silent, he gestured at me with his gun. "You are not drinking your scotch. Were you not so thirsty after all?" He raised an eyebrow. He'd finished his first glass already.

I'd forgotten about it, to be honest. Looking down at the glass, I lifted it to my lips and sipped, letting it glide down my throat like fiery velvet. Being drunk wasn't a good idea, but something to take the edge off wasn't necessarily a bad idea. "I'm afraid I'm off my routine. Your unexpected visit caught me off guard."

"Again, I like your style, Mr. Porter." He nodded slowly as he took a sip of his drink as well, sighing lustily in appreciation.

Nice to know he enjoyed the scotch. The shit cost more than a thousand dollars a bottle. Not that I couldn't afford it, but I didn't really want to waste that kind of money on someone who was probably considering where in my body was the best place to put a bullet.

The Russian mafia, sitting in my penthouse, and drinking my Macallan. If someone back in Chicago had told me that this was where I'd end up, I never would've believed him.

He swirled the dark amber liquid in the glass as he studied me over the rim of the cut crystal. "You know, a man like you could be useful to us...if you can convince your client to plead out. You don't get nervous. You don't get..." He waved a hand in the air. "Panicky. I had a man once, he screamed like a little girl when I pulled a gun on him. Fucking pathetic. Annoyed the shit out of me. Pissed his pants before I shot him."

"Glad I'm not...annoying the shit out of you." Had I hit that key fob? Was it working? Would the cops get here?

He grinned at me, showing me brilliant teeth in a sharp smile. "I hear sarcasm in your voice, Mr. Porter. Sharp, smart – you have balls." He leaned back a bit but there was nothing relaxed about that pose. "Would you like to be useful to us, Mr. Porter? To me? To my boss? I could make calls."

"No." I replied without even blinking an eye.

I didn't even have to think about it. Aside from the fact that there was no way I wanted this bastard coming back here, there was no way in hell I was going to work for the mob. I'd just as soon he put a bullet in my head right now.

I kept my tone as polite as possible. "Let me be clear, Mr...well...sir, I'd like to be very clear. Hell, no. I don't want any misunderstandings."

To my surprise, he laughed. I didn't really see the humor in it, but who was I to tell him he couldn't find this amusing.

A bead of sweat rolled down the back of my neck and I swallowed again, the tension in my neck so heavy now, I thought it might crack if I even turned my head. The alcohol wasn't really doing a whole lot to relax me. Or, if it was, I wouldn't want to know how strung out I'd be without it.

"You want to be clear, hmm. No misunderstandings? Smart man." He nodded. "You do not wish to get...involved in certain elements. I understand this. I am not surprised. You are smart. It is..." He paused, his brow crumpling as though he was searching for the word. Then he smiled. "Okay. It is okay. There are other people we use, better probably. They are predictable. You are not. You are smart, and smart is always good. But predictable is better. I know a lost cause when I see one."

He came out of his seat then, that gun loosely held at his side.

I didn't let myself look at it, as much as I wanted to. No. I didn't *want* to. It was that my gaze felt *drawn* to the weapon. But I didn't think that was a good idea.

He took another step toward me, and I tried to decide which was going to be my best bet, grab for the gun or try to get out of the way.

The landline rang.

It surprised me enough to distract me from the gun, and this time, I couldn't stop myself from looking at the object that held my interest. From looking at the phone, sitting innocuously on my counter, waiting for me to pick it up and answer.

The damn thing hardly ever rang. I had the cellphone, and used it more often than not. But sometimes, cell phones didn't work. Storms had knocked cellular service out more than once, even in the city, and I'd learned early on to have a more reliable way to stay connected with the world.

However, the worst thing I could have done was *react* to it.

In the months I'd been in New York, that landline had rang maybe five times.

Why in the hell was it ringing now?

The hitman noticed my attention, and his brows arched. With a smile curling his lips, he walked over, cutting a wide circle that kept me in his line of sight as he moved to the phone. He held my eyes as he picked it up, a different kind of amusement in his gaze. In the other hand, he lifted the weapon, pointing it at me.

"Hello, Mr. Porter's residence. Can I help you?"

In the faint pause that followed, I could make out nothing about who was on the other side. He was too far away and the caller spoke too quietly. A part of me wasn't sure I wanted to know, because if it was someone I cared about, I didn't know how I'd react.

Though who would...?

Shit. Dena.

If that was her...

My stomach clenched.

"No, I'm sorry," he said, head cocked. "I'm a friend. I'm afraid Mr. Porter is indisposed for the next few minutes. May I take a message? He will be back presently."

The man sounded like a damn diplomat's personal assistant. He barely had an accent at all.

Amusement glinted in his eyes as he looked over at me. "Oh, hello, Mrs. Pott – oh, *Miss* Pott, I apologize. May I say, you have a very...no, forgive me. That is inappropriate. I just feel as though I know you because Mr. Porter speaks of you so often."

Jaw clenched, I fought not to come off the chair and go after him. The only thing that stopped me was the fact that I wasn't bullet proof, or faster than a fucking bullet. My assistant at the firm seemed competent. She was certainly eager to prove herself to me. I just hoped she was smart enough to not give out any important personal information to the schmuck on the phone.

Although chances were, the hitman knew more than I wanted him to anyway. I wouldn't have exactly counted Ella Pott as someone I cared about, but she wasn't someone I wanted to see hurt. I needed to get out of here.

"In answer to your question, I'm a friend of Arik's. Yes, we go way back. I'm just in the area for the evening – dropped in to ask for a favor and a..." He swirled the scotch around in a glass and smiled. "Drink. He had to step out to take a call. Business related. Shall I take a message?"

A few moments later, he hung up. He'd delicately tried to push for more information from her.

He'd failed.

I'd be giving Ms. Pott a bonus.

Assuming, of course, that I lived.

"She is very professional." He returned to his seat, the weapon lifted and pointed dead at my forehead once more. "You should give her a bonus."

I didn't like how his thoughts echoed mine so closely, but I managed a casual shrug. "I should. Good help isn't always easy to come by."

When he grinned at me, I decided that I wanted to see him choking on that shit-eating grin. Hitmen really shouldn't be so easily amused, especially not when they're contemplating how to kill you.

"She says that a woman called for you." He really seemed to be enjoying himself now. "Said she was from the DA's office and needed to speak to you. I wonder who that could have been."

Dena.

I forced myself to keep very still, not wanting to give him the slightest hint that I cared.

"It's getting late," I said.

"It is," he agreed. "Let's get back to business then." He leaned forward, the gun dangling negligently between his knees.

Yet again, I wasn't disarmed by his supposed lack of caution. His eyes were far too alert for him to *not* be paying attention to everything. I assumed that he wouldn't still be alive if he wasn't good at his job. I felt pretty certain that most hit-men who were distracted rarely lived long.

Case in point, his eyes shot to the door almost a second before the knock came.

"You are a busy man for somebody who didn't seem to be aware he had plans this evening, Mr. Porter," he muttered, looking vaguely disgusted for the first time that evening. As he rose again, he looked over at me. "Were you expecting company?"

I shook my head. Keeping my voice low, I said, "Ignore it. They probably have the wrong apartment. Whoever it is will go away."

I hoped so anyway. I could only think of one person who knew about this place. I hadn't finished moving in until a couple days ago.

He ran his tongue across his teeth as he flicked his eyes between the door and me.

The knock came again.

Slowly, he walked over and looked into the hallway. "It's a woman. She is pretty." He glanced at me. "I know her, Mr. Porter."

Shit.

He walked partway back toward me and spoke in a low voice. "It is the assistant DA. Perhaps she is the one who called your Miss Pott. I have seen you with her."

The smile told me that he didn't just mean in the courtroom.

"You...well, you have an interesting relationship with her, do you not? And Bethany McDermott? She doesn't like her at all."

"Fuck Bethany McDermott," I said before I could stop myself.

His lips rolled in like he was suppressing a laugh.

The knock hadn't come again.

Blowing out a slow breath, I hoped that meant Dena had left. I needed her to be safe. More than my own life, I wanted her to be safe.

But just as I started to relax, her voice rang out.

"Arik? Are you in there? I need to talk to you."

"She'll go away," I said again, making it more firm this time, as if that would make a difference. *Go away, Dena... please*

But he was already walking to the door. "I don't think I want her to."

My body tensed and I half-rose, already prepared to shout out a warning. But he had his gun lifted, pointed to the door. If he squeezed the trigger...I had good security, but I didn't know how well the door would hold up to a bullet.

Slowly, I lowered myself back into the seat, and when he opened the door, I saw her.

My heart seemed to freeze inside my chest.

This couldn't be happening.

I almost turned to leave after he didn't answer the second knock. But I didn't have any place else to go other than home. Leslie would have no problem with me staying with her for a couple days, but it wasn't like she lived in some heavily guarded building with bulky security guards. I knew Club Privé was open, and that all I'd have to do is go there and tell Carrie and Gavin that I was worried, but I didn't want to put this on them. Gavin was the type who'd want to take charge, and that would make him a target.

I didn't want to put them in danger.

But, apparently, I had no problem putting Arik in danger.

I might've been a horrible person for it, but instead of turning away, I called out. "Arik? Are you in there? I need to talk to you."

Several more seconds passed without an answer, and I started to turn away, certain that he'd chosen to ignore me, but then the doorknob turned. The memory of our last encounter was all that kept me from taking an immediate step toward him.

Except it wasn't Arik standing there.

I recognized those eyes right away, and I supposed that was

one of the things that saved me. That, and the fact that I hadn't taken that step toward the door. A few moments ago, I'd been standing right there, but now, with a distance of a few feet between me and him, I had a precious split second for my brain and body to react.

My brain screamed *shit*, but my gut took over. Later, I'd have to thank my dad for insisting I take some seriously grueling self-defense courses once he realized I was serious about going into criminal law.

I was far from tall or muscular, but I knew how to use what I did have. What I had was the knowledge that my legs were the most powerful muscles in my body, and when he went to reach for me, I moved *toward* him instead of away as he probably expected.

It also helped that he was partially behind the door, because that was where I kicked. I kicked straight at it, snapping out with my knee the way I'd learned. I hadn't gone to class in years, but I'd studied throughout middle and high school, and muscle memory was a beautiful thing. The door drove back into him and he grunted. With a gliding little half-hop, I kicked forward again, driving him back farther, and battering him with the door a second time.

That was when somebody else joined the fight, ramming the stranger into the wall.

Something clattered on the floor and, instinctively, I kicked at it before I even realized it was a gun. It slid away as I squeezed myself in through the tight space allowed by the two struggling bodies.

Arik drove a fist into the man's face hard enough to make me wince.

He spewed out something ugly in a harsh, deep language – Russian, I thought. Of course it was Russian. I knew who he was now, and he sure as hell wasn't murmuring sweet nothings in French.

While my mind kept up the strange babbling, another part of me stepped up and took over. I didn't feel like *me* as I bent down and grabbed the gun, and I sure as *hell* didn't feel like me as I gripped it and checked the safety. It had been on. How weird was that?

But it didn't matter the reasoning. What mattered was that, even though I'd never owned a gun or intended to own one, a couple years ago, I'd taken a gun safety course and done some target practicing.

When the hitman managed to flip his way on top of Arik, I stepped closer and pressed the nose of the gun to the back of his head.

My voice was as cold as I'd ever heard it. "Safety's off now."

He froze.

A split second later, a weird, whining noise escaped his throat, and he rolled off to the side, curled in on himself and clutching at his crotch. People rarely acknowledged that, in a life-or-death situation, even a man will knee another man in the balls.

Arik sat up, panting. His nose was bleeding, his bottom lip split. He looked at me as he staggered upright, the concern on his face focused all on me. When he took a step toward me, hand outstretched as if to take the gun, I backed up.

"I think I can handle the fucking gun. Why don't you tie him up or something?"

Arik's eyes widened slightly, but I didn't really care about his surprise at the moment. I wanted to make sure the man on the ground didn't sense a moment of hesitation.

"The...little girl...thinks she can...handle a gun." The hitman wheezed out a laugh.

"Fuck off," I snapped. I'd always prided myself on my levelheadedness, but that part of my self-control had snapped at some point in the last few hours.

The hitman rolled onto one knee and I shifted, making sure the gun was still aimed at him.

"Give me the gun. I'll go. My...business here is done."

"I'm curious about that." Off to the side, Arik was rummaging around in nearby drawers.

I couldn't figure out what was taking him so long. He had to have something here he could use. The man was a Dom for fuck's sake!

Then it hit me. All of Arik's bondage things were in his bedroom or playroom, not out here. And he apparently didn't want to leave the room. It almost made me laugh.

The hitman shifted again, bringing my thoughts back to the present. I knew I was dangerously close to going into shock. I needed to focus on something, anything, to keep my head on straight.

"While we're waiting, why don't you tell me about those plans, and maybe about your relationship with my boss?"

His eyelids flickered and he tensed. For a moment, I thought he was going to come after me, then his mouth opened slightly as he started to say something.

Whatever those words were, however, died when Arik smashed something heavy down on his head. I figured out what it was a moment later when the potent fumes of whiskey flooded the air. The hitman slumped forward, his eyes rolling toward the back of his skull.

Over the unconscious body, Arik looked up at me. His emerald gaze burned, his chest heaved. "Unconscious is just as good as tied up, right?" He swiped at the blood on his face and took a half step toward me.

I swallowed and looked away. "We need to call the..."

"Police!"

"Mr. Porter, we received–"

"Ma'am, drop the gun, hands up!"

"Oh, for crying out loud."

Lifting one hand into the air, I knelt down and put the gun on the now-blood splattered carpet. Idly, I wondered how much it would cost to clean it, or if Arik would just have it replaced. Pity. The place was so new.

Arik spoke up as he edged toward me. "Officers, you're holding a weapon on the wrong person. This is ADA Dena Monroe..."

As he started to explain, I closed my eyes and tried to deal with the spinning in my head.

This was going to prove to be one long, long night.

———

ONE OF THE officers approached me as I stood in the kitchen drinking water a few minutes later.

"I'm sorry about..." He gestured toward the door.

Shaking my head, I said, "You're doing your job. Security alert, unknown person holding a weapon...you did what you're trained to do."

He nodded. "Appreciate the understanding, Miss Monroe. Mr. Porter explained everything to us, but I'll need to take your statement as well."

I really didn't want to go over anything, but I knew procedure. "Of course."

We were only halfway through my explanation of what had happened – with the careful but legal exclusion of the fact that I'd seen the hitman fucking my boss earlier this week – when there was another knock on the somewhat askew door. Between me kicking it and Arik's unexpected guest shoving back, even its excellent construction hadn't been able to hold up. It was a good thing Arik's family owned the building. Otherwise, that would've been a bitch to try to explain.

The new addition didn't bother to introduce himself or be invited inside.

"I'll be running the investigation from here on out," he announced.

I stood to the side and listened as he walked around, introducing himself to the officers, to Arik. Based on the way he was carrying himself, Lieutenant Beale considered his presence to be quite important.

I already didn't like him.

When he paused by the suspect, a faint smirk curved his lips and he shook his head.

"Always knew that arrogance would trip you up sooner or later."

The now semi-coherent hitman sneered, but didn't say anything.

Lieutenant Beale came toward me at last. "Ms. Monroe, I take it?"

I glanced down at his hand and debated shaking it. Then I reminded myself that I was an ADA and there was no reason to be rude. I'd probably have to work with this man at some point and he hadn't really done anything that deserved my dislike. His grasp was firm, precise, like he'd practiced the perfect handshake.

"I take it you're in the middle of giving your statement?" The smile that came with the question was close-lipped and didn't reach his eyes.

"Yes." I pushed a hand through my hair, and tried not to sigh. "I take it I need to start all over?"

"It would simplify things."

I looked at the water I was still drinking. Taking a sip, I said,

"I'm still a little shocky. I need the fluids, Lieutenant. Give me a minute and I'll start this all over again."

"I hate to be an inconvenience." The corner of his mouth hitched up in a smile more infuriating than the last. "But it's useful, as you are probably aware, to get solid facts. The sooner we can get this done, the sooner you can go home."

Asshole. I took another sip of my water, half out of spite, and when I lowered the glass, my hand shook badly enough that I spilled the liquid across my hand and arm.

The officer I'd originally been talking to handed me a paper towel.

"Thanks." I gave him a grateful look and then looked at the lieutenant.

"Miss Monroe," Lieutenant Beale said my name, as if reminding me that he was still here. And that I was wasting his time.

That thin veneer of control I'd managed to get back in the last few minutes cracked. "I'm so sorry, Lieutenant, if I'm being an inconvenience. Please excuse me." Sarcasm dripped off of every word. "I mean, it's not like I've never had a gun pointed at me, or had to point a gun at someone else. I'm sure every native New Yorker or ADA has been in this situation numerous times. I'll try to get my shit together."

Lieutenant Beale's eyes narrowed even as color crept up his neck and cheeks. "Why don't you do that?" He yanked his phone out of his pocket. "I'm going to call 1PP to give them an update." He stalked away.

"Excuse Lieutenant Beale," the officer next to me said. "He's only on the force to meet the asshole quota, Ms. Monroe." He gave me a grin. "That or the dick quota. Actually, I think he meets both."

I smiled to show him I appreciated the support. Then my

eyes met Arik's and I saw that he didn't think any of this was funny either.

IT TOOK FOREVER for Lieutenant Beale to finish taking my statement, and an equally long time for him to finish with Arik. I was pretty sure he was dragging it out intentionally. By the time it was all said and done, I wanted to collapse. Actually, I pretty much *did*. Sitting on Arik's couch, my legs curled up beneath me, my eyes had drooped closed, and the next thing I knew, Arik was rubbing my shoulder.

"Dena."

Jerking upright, I automatically swung for the person touching me.

He caught my wrist, his grip firm, but not rough. He gave me a wry smile as his thumb brushed across my racing pulse-point. "I've got to tell you, Councilor. That's one hell of a right hook you've got."

Staring at him, aware of the fact that more than a few of the officers were watching with varying degrees of interest, I jerked on my wrist.

"Sorry," I muttered, embarrassment making my voice sharp. Blood rushed to my face as I stood up and took a few unsteady steps off to the side. "I'm a little...jumpy."

"Understandable." One of the cops moved between us and gave me a professional smile. He wasn't the one I'd given my statement to, but he seemed just as nice. "We were just telling Mr. Porter that he'd have to pack up for a few days. I doubt there's much evidence to collect, but the techs will have to go through. And..."

His eyes slid to the hitman.

His name. I knew his name, but I couldn't think of it.

Shock, I told myself. Shock, exhaustion. Both.

As the officer caught my eyes, I nodded. I understood what he'd been saying. If the Russian mafia knew where Arik was, then it wasn't safe for him to come back here for a few days.

A shiver raced down my spine, and I had to wonder if it was safe at my place.

"I've got somewhere to go," Arik said, distracting the officers as I turned away. They spoke for a few more minutes as I wandered over to the large, floor to ceiling windows that ran the length of the living room. My body tightened as I remembered what happened the last time I'd been here.

I wanted to tell him to come home with me, that I didn't want to be alone. That I wanted him to be with me.

But it was probably a bad idea to say that in front of an audience. Especially an audience who I might see again for work.

It didn't take long for everybody to clear out once the cops made it clear we wouldn't be left alone inside the apartment. Reluctantly, I bit my tongue and didn't say anything to Arik as we walked out. From the hallway, I watched as the officers placed bright yellow crime scene tape over the door.

We rode down to the lobby in two silent parties, Beale and half the uniforms with the now-upright cuffed suspect going first. His eyes glittered at me before the elevator door closed, blocking him from sight. By the time we reached the lobby, he was already being hustled out to an unmarked, flanked by two black and whites, their lights flashing in the pouring rain, but I could still feel his eyes on me.

"Make sure you let us know of your whereabouts, Mr. Porter," one of the officers said to Arik.

"My office will be able to contact me if you need me." His voice was polite, but purposely vague.

I knew he wouldn't be telling anybody anything. Judging by the expression on the young cop's face, he knew it too, but he didn't press. As glad as I'd been to see them arrive, I couldn't deny the relief at seeing them go.

When we were alone in the lobby, Arik finally turned to me.

I opened my mouth to tell him he could come stay with me, even though part of me was still angry, still hurt. We'd figure that part out later. Right now, I just couldn't deal with being alone.

He put his finger over my lips, effectively stopping the flow of words before they even started. A faint smile cracked his lips and he quirked an eyebrow. "Remind me to never get on the wrong side of a door with you."

I started to answer, but all that came out was a shaky sigh.

In the next minute, I was caught up in his arms. His lips brushed my temple as he whispered, "I don't think I've ever been that scared before."

"Don't go to a hotel," I said quietly, all but desperate now. My arms were around his waist, and I knew I should be embarrassed at the way I was clinging to him, but I couldn't manage to feel any of that at the moment. "Come home with me."

"Don't go home," he said in return. "Come with me."

I pulled back, staring up at him. He brushed my hair back from my face. "He knows who you are, Dena. He recognized you."

That very thought made my heart pound and I sucked in oxygen, although it didn't seem to reach my lungs. Or maybe the blood wasn't reaching my brain. Either way, I felt lightheaded and queasy.

"He...he what?"

"He knows who you are." Gently, Arik cupped my cheek, his thumb rubbing back and forth over my bottom lip. "Come with me. I want you to be safe."

"And go where? To a hotel? Is *that* safe?" I asked, only half-joking. Every bad movie I'd ever seen with shoot-ups in hotel hallways started to flash through my mind. Even less comforting was that most of them dealt with people trying to hide from the mob.

"We're not going to a hotel. We're going someplace I *know* is safe." He dropped his hand so that both of his arms were around me again.

I stared up at him, my brain struggling to keep up with all of the reasons why this wasn't a good idea. Even if I had been the one who'd originally suggested it. "We shouldn't. The case... everything. This is stupid."

"Do you care?" he asked, eyes intense as they cut into me.

"Do you?" I countered.

"You have an annoying habit of answering questions with questions." Arik bent his head, pressed his lips to mine in a firm but chaste, kiss. "But no. I don't care. Right now, the only thing I care about is having you some place safe." His voice lowered to that tone I'd already come to recognize. "Once I have you safe, I plan on getting you naked and under me."

"That..." Some of the knots inside me started to relax, and I blew out a breath. Fuck it. I'd played by the rules my whole life and I needed this. Needed him. "That sounds like a good plan. Even if it is stupid. And no, I don't think I care if it's stupid."

"Neither do I."

He curled an arm around my waist and we started for the door. "For the record, if you'd insisted on going back to your place, I would have been parked in a car out front the rest of the night. Just so you know."

"Stalker, much?" I managed a half-teasing smile.

"If that's what it takes to keep you safe," he said.

I curled into him as he led me out into the rain, the warmth of his words protecting me from the chill of the night.

EIGHTEEN

DENA

The towering, imposing structure jutted overhead as we climbed out of the car. It was made of old stone, the kind you didn't see very often any more. This was the furthest thing from Arik's place in the city that I'd seen. If the circumstances had been different, I would've been more impressed and less feeling like this entire thing was becoming more surreal by the moment. The fact that it was nearly one in the morning after the hardest day I'd ever had wasn't helping matters much.

"What did you do, bring me to Frankenstein's lair?" I asked, shoving my damp hair back. I'd been too distracted to get a trim recently and my hair was longer than I usually liked it.

A man was already at the curb, holding out an umbrella, but I wasn't much in the mood to have somebody at my elbow, so I waved him off as I climbed out of the car. Rain now plastered my hair to my skull as I looked over at Arik.

He was also staring up at the house, and a faint smile curled his lips. "Welcome to my home away from home, Dena."

This was definitely not what I'd been expecting. We'd taken his car since he hadn't trusted a cab driver not to share information with anyone who paid enough, but he hadn't told me where he was taking me. There'd been twists and turns that I wasn't sure were necessary, but were rather his way of guaranteeing that we weren't being followed.

"Marcum," Arik said, nodding at the man with the umbrella as we began walking toward the house.

It sounded much classier than Jeeves, although not as cool as Alfred. If he'd been an Alfred, then I could have teased Arik about taking me to the bat cave. It hit me in that moment just how exhausted I must be, standing in the grand foyer of this insane house, making internal Batman jokes while the man I was...whatever with quietly chatted with a couple of others – and he had blood on his suit.

Blood. From fighting with Mr. Russian Mafia Hitman. Some of it was the other guy's...but some of it was Arik's.

A shudder wracked me and it had little to do with how cold I was. I turned away from him, pressing the tips of my fingers to my lips before the low noise building in my throat could escape. Just outside the heavy oak doors and the thick frosted glass, the rain pounded down even harder and I was actually tempted to step out into it, wondering if maybe that would wash away the shock of the night.

Would I be able to go back to my place in Chelsea tomorrow? Or any time soon? Had Bethany been tipped off? Did she know I'd been at Arik's when her 'friend' had paid him a visit? Could somebody be watching me even now, having somehow tracked us down?

I just didn't know.

Something hit me then. The call I'd gotten in the cab. Had it really been some random thing? Or had that scream on the other end, the one that had ended the call, had that been someone I knew? I thought, when I'd gotten it, that it had been Arik. Then when I'd gotten to the apartment, I all but forgot about it. Now, however, I couldn't help but wonder if it had been Bethany.

Thinking of her was like a splash of cold water in my face, and I reached for my phone, needing for the police to know. I wasn't going to call that asshole lieutenant though. I was going to call someone I trusted.

Despite the late hour, Officer Dunne answered. I gave him the quick, short version, as well as the name of the lieutenant. He promised to look into it, and reminded me to be careful.

I'd just hung up when Arik came over. "Dena, I'm so sorry. You're standing out here soaked after everything that's happened."

As his voice trailed off, I turned to look at him. "Don't apologize. I needed to make a call anyway." I paused, and then added, "I'll tell you later."

I had to tell him about it, about Bethany, and her connection to the man in his apartment. But not now, even if he asked.

He looked like he wanted to say more, but instead, he just nodded and held out a hand. "We'll sleep in my old room."

"Your old room?" I asked.

As he led me deeper inside the house, I tried to see everything, if only for the distraction. The house was...posh. Opulent, over the top and *posh*. I couldn't think of a better way to describe it. I'd known Arik came from money, and that his father had invested in property in the city. I just hadn't realized they had a house like this nearby.

"So is this where you spent long, boring old summers while your parents were out yachting or something?"

A quick grin flashed across his face. "No. I had a place like that, but it was in upper Michigan. Not quite as far from Chicago as New York." The smile faded as we mounted the stairs. "This place...well, it belonged to a relative. It's ours now."

As we climbed the stairs, he placed a hand on my lower

spine. I lost track of the halls, the turns, the twists. After what seemed like an endless journey, we were in a massive, elegantly decorated room, and I turned, facing Arik once more. "So you have this...and that place in the city?"

"Sort of." He tucked his hands into his pockets, looking around. "This isn't mine. It's my dad's, more or less. But it's safe, and that's all that matters for now."

He rubbed a hand back and forth over his damp hair, droplets flying everywhere. "This place...well, nobody's lived here other than the household staff for years. I think Dad and I stayed here maybe three times in twice as many years."

"And we're here now because...?"

"I already told you." Flat, simple words. "It's safe."

He turned away and moved to the window. I followed him, staring outside and wondering what it was he saw. Despite everything going on around us, I knew that something wasn't right. There was an ache of sadness in the air, and I knew it had something to do with this place.

"What happened here?"

"That," Arik said in a heavy voice. "Would depend on who you ask. But I don't want to talk about that tonight."

He turned back to me and reached out, drawing me to him.

The warmth of his body bled into my cold one, making me shiver. He felt so good, so steady and strong. Through his damp clothes, the heat of him was like a furnace and I was drawn to it. I wanted to rest my head on his chest, but stopped, staring at the blood on his shirtfront.

I braced a hand a few inches below the stains, wondering how much of it was his, thinking about how close the both of us had come to getting seriously hurt. How close we'd come to dying.

Arik restlessly rubbed his hands up and down my hips. "I can't tell you how scared I was when I realized it was you at the door, Dena. And when he made it clear he knew who you were..." His fingers flexed even as his eyes darkened.

He dipped his head, pressed his lips to mine. He didn't deepen the kiss, just stood there, as if he needed the reassurance of my presence as much as I needed his. I slid my hands up and cupped his face, feeling the abrasive scratch of five o'clock shadow against my hands. My entire body throbbed at the thought of how that would feel against the insides of my thighs.

I broke the kiss, but kept my forehead pressed against his. "I've been trying to tell myself that I'm not ready to talk to you yet, that I need to think things through more." I closed my eyes. "I want to be mad at you, but I can't."

"I can't either," he admitted.

I opened my eyes, meeting his emerald ones. I lowered my hands, and stared at the splatters of blood on his clothes. Suddenly desperate to be rid of all reminders of the evening, I pushed at his suit jacket.

"There's blood on you." My voice was shaking. Normally, that would have pissed me off, but I didn't care at the moment.

Once I had his jacket on the floor, I reached for his tie. My fingers fumbled for a moment, then his hands covered mine, stilling the restless movement. Then he was easily taking care of the knot while I started on the buttons of his no longer pristine white shirt.

He left me to it, his hands returning to my hips once he'd finished with the tie, but once I reached for the buckle of his belt, he stopped me.

"Now you," he said, his voice gruff.

It was my turn to stand there, unmoving as he stripped off my shirt and bra. He paused a moment as I shivered, then dipped his head and closed his lips around a nipple that had gone tight with cold and need. The exquisite contrast between my chilled flesh and his hot mouth had me moaning.

He did nothing but that. One deep, drawing tug of my nipple between his lips and then he went back to stripping me bare.

Once I was completely naked, he picked me up and carried me across the room.

Not to the bed, though.

There was a fireplace, and after he'd laid me down on a thick rug, covered me with a nearby blanket, then turned to the cold hearth. Within a few moments, he had a blaze going.

"You're good at that." My voice shook. I don't know if it was cold, nerves, or need...or all of them above.

He stretched out next to me and tossed the blanket aside. "Stop talking."

He didn't give me a chance to argue, covering my mouth with his. I moaned as his tongue slid into my mouth. A moment later, he moved over me, his skin hot against mine. He'd stripped his trousers away without me even noticing, and it was all bare flesh to bare flesh. I didn't even know how he managed to generate so much heat after the rain, but I didn't really care.

I wanted more of him – a lot more.

Bringing my knees up, I rubbed against him, felt the length of his cock pulsing against me. Arik caught my wrists and drew them over my head, staring down at me with hungry eyes.

"I don't want to play tonight," I warned him. "I need this – need you – too much."

"I'm not playing." His voice had that low, authoritative note to it that made my insides squirm. Then he drove inside me with one single thrust. I cried out from the suddenness of it.

He didn't give me any time to adjust either, simply withdrawing and then surging forward again, deep and hard and fast. Bracing my heels on the floor, I lifted up to meet him. I wanted it to ride that line of almost-pain. I wanted something that would obliterate everything else. Shatter everything that wasn't him and me.

Arik kissed me then, a bruising, carnal kiss that filled all the dark and cold places, eased every unspoken fear. His cock filled me, the kiss, savage as it was, soothed me. It was almost too much for me to handle, but I clung to it. Clung to every sensation.

He was here. I was here.

We were together and that was what mattered.

He tore his mouth away and lifted his head, staring at me with eyes glittering with something dark and somehow...full.

"Don't ever scare me like that again," he said, his voice harsh, commanding.

I nodded, nearly whimpering as I ground against him.

He kissed me again, just as hard, just as deep. Just as fierce and hungry.

"Say it, Dena. Say it," he rasped against my lips.

"I won't scare you like that again." Then, before he could break the kiss, I bit his lower lip, hard. His hips jerked against me, driving deeper. He made a sound like a growl.

"Now you," I said, the words breathless.

He understood. His body covered mine fully as he murmured against my mouth. "I won't scare you like that again."

His strokes slowed, gentled, and he let go of my wrists to push up onto his knees. I was warmer now, but I still missed the warmth of him. His large hands cupped my breasts, thumbs circling my nipples while he rolled his hips lazily against the cradle of mine. His cock, thick and hard, pulsed inside me, and I could feel the climax building.

He slid his hands over my legs, then his hands between my thighs to where we joined. "I've missed this," he murmured, stroking my sensitive skin. "Having you with me, feeling you wrapped around my dick. I've missed that smart mouth, those beautiful eyes."

I wanted to say something to him, tell him I'd missed him too. But the feel of him pumping inside me, the way he watched me, and the way he spoke – he shattered me in ways nobody else ever had, ever could.

"Arik..."

I came then, a slow, sweet climax so at odds with the vicious need that had fueled this.

As though he'd just been waiting for it, Arik bent over me again, and thrust hard, once...twice...three times before he joined me, his entire body shuddering with the force of his orgasm.

I wrapped my arms around him and held tight, wanting to keep his body curled around me. For those few moments, all the insanity of the day faded.

This was all that mattered.

We – whatever we were – were all that mattered.

It ought to have been downright criminal to be awake at this hour, especially considering I hadn't even managed to get to sleep until after two. But the silvery moonlight coming in through the window fell on the antique clock hanging on the wall, clearly showed me the ungodly time of four fifty-two.

I might have had a little over two hours of sleep, and I was now wide awake. There was absolutely no chance in hell I'd be getting back to sleep either. My brain was already working overtime.

The soft, warm body next to me stirred, and I turned my head, staring at the shadowed outline of Dena's face. I had one quick glimpse of her before she shifted and wiggled deeper into the covers. A low, unhappy sound escaped her, telling me that while she was still sleeping, her rest was far from *restful*.

That bothered me more than I thought it would.

If I stayed there, I was going to wake her.

I blew out a breath. There was no point in both of us being tired, exhausted messes when we finally managed to have our talk.

Climbing out of bed, I rummaged through the dresser in the

dark. Although I rarely came here, I'd always kept clothing on hand. With only a little difficulty, I managed to find a pair of jeans and an old T-shirt. After I pulled them on, I moved to the window and stared out into the early morning. I'd grown up in the city and it still amazed me sometimes how different things looked in the dark when there weren't any city lights around.

I'd had a relatively easy life. A happy one, even. There had been one dark period, a mar in my teens, and that was what had driven me to law.

That dark period was also tied to this house, and coming back here was never...easy.

But that one incident hadn't permanently scarred or warped me, turned me into a closed-off loner. It hadn't even really made me hate this place, even with the darkness. Things had always been fairly easy for me too. I was smart, successful, and never looking for anything even close to romantically complicated.

The emotions I was dealing with now, however, were the kind I'd never had to deal with before, at least not on this level.

Rage, fear, doubt...guilt wanted to come in and play too. Not to mention all the self-recriminations for everything that happened, but I wasn't going to start beating myself up over what I couldn't change. I couldn't afford to, because if I let anything trip me up, next time I might not come out on top.

Next time Dena and I might not survive.

Dena...that single thought pushed me into an ugly spiral, and I dropped into a chair, staring at nothing while I relived each and every moment from the night before. I didn't know how long I spent trapped in my own thoughts, or how I might have stayed there, if Dena hadn't stirred, a soft, shaky sigh coming from the bed.

Pulling myself out of the reverie, I looked over at her just as she started to stretch.

Fuck, she was hot.

When she rolled onto her belly and turned her head toward me, one hand sliding down the empty space where I had been sleeping next to her, I rose from the chair. I wasn't about to let her get the wrong idea.

She was pushing herself up onto her elbows as I settled down on the edge of the bed. I caught her hand in mine and lifted it to my lips. Some of that white blonde hair fell into her eyes as a sleepy, sexy smile curved her mouth.

It was in that moment, as I felt all the fear inside me melt away, replaced by a gut-wrenching warmth and need, that I let myself finally admit the truth. I had gone and fallen for her.

I could have lost her. Just the thought made me feel sick. Turning her palm upward, I pressed a kiss to the center and whispered her name.

I crawled across the bed toward her and caught her up against me, holding her. Her back to my front, I buried my face in her hair and just held on tight, needing that vital, physical reminder that we were both here, that she hadn't been hurt. That I hadn't lost her.

That it wasn't too late to figure out what was going on with us. After all we'd been through, I couldn't lose her just because I'd been an ass.

Rubbing my cheek against hers, I said softly, "We need to talk."

"I know." She craned her head around and pressed a quick, soft kiss to my lips. "That's why I came over last night in the first place."

For a second, I didn't get what she meant, and then I laughed, pressing my face into her hair as I understood. Dammit. At least she wasn't still pissed at me. That meant what I had could wait.

"I'm talking personal stuff. I get the feeling you aren't, are you?"

"No." She wiggled around and stared at me, her face solemn in the dim light. "Personal stuff? Did last night finally convince you that this really *is* a bad idea?"

Her voice was light, teasing. But there was an edge to her words. My heart twisted in a way I'd never felt before.

"No." Leaning over, I pressed my lips to hers. "No."

A shaky sigh escaped her lips, but I couldn't tell what it meant.

"Then you must want to have a...relationship talk."

"You're a sharp woman, Dena Monroe. That's really sexy." I grinned.

She bit my lower lip. Heat tightened in me, but before I could do much about it, she pulled away, taking most of the covers with her as she slid off the bed. As she moved over to the window, I drew one knee up and braced an elbow on it, watching her.

Fuck, I could spend all day just watching her.

"I'm going to go first," she said softly. "You're right, you know. We do need to talk, but there's...shit. Things are a fucking shit-storm, and personal things will have to wait. Especially after last night."

When she turned to look at me, the expression in her eyes made the tension inside me expand. Instantly, I pushed everything else aside and focused on whatever it was she needed to tell me.

"What's going on?"

Dena tipped her head back. "What's going on?" she murmured, echoing my question. "Where do I start?"

She rolled her head back and forth, then reached up to rub at her neck. The blankets she had gripped in one fist sagged, allowing a glimpse of one small, firm breast. I had to force my eyes back up to her face. I knew whatever she had to say was important, but I was only human.

"I'm about to do something that's toeing the line on some ethical boundaries, Arik. We're not going to talk about the case, so we're not quite at that crossing point, but what I'm about to tell you..."

She lapsed into silence then, and when she didn't say anything else for a couple of minutes, I cleared my throat and she lifted an eyebrow.

"Maybe you could sit down with me while you talk," I suggested. Sliding my gaze down, then back up, I added, "You did kind of steal all of my covers."

"You're dressed," she said easily.

But then she shrugged and came back to me, so I was content. I tugged her down to straddle me and she wrapped the blankets around us both, curling one arm around my neck. She didn't lean into me, though. She kept a few inches between us and her eyes stayed on mine.

"I knew the guy in your apartment," she said, worrying her lower lip with her teeth. "I saw him and I knew him. The cops, they told you who he was, right?"

"Yeah," I said. I was really hoping that the reason she knew him was because he was a wanted criminal and that was sort of her department. I brushed her hair back from her face. "I might be from Chicago, but I've never had to deal with the mafia before."

"You don't understand, Arik. It wasn't the first time I've seen him."

Now she leaned in, pressing her forehead to mine. Her voice, her eyes, everything about her was intense, and I had a sudden flash of how she would look in court. Damn, if she put that much passion into her cases – and I knew she did – she'd be a formidable foe.

Then she was speaking again. "It took me days to place him, but last night, I figured it out."

Again, she stopped.

I knew the expression on her face. It was the one somebody wore when they were piecing together a puzzle, and it looked like hers had a lot of pieces. Resting one hand on her thigh, I stroked up and down, and told myself I was doing a damn good job of not letting her see that I wanted to ask clarifying questions.

She'd *seen* him?

What the fuck, and where the fuck?

Had he threatened her?

Would he have hurt her?

The thought made something vicious, something I'd never felt before, rise up inside me.

Caught up in my own thoughts, when Dena started to talk again, it took me a minute to process anything she said.

"...late, almost everybody was gone..."

Giving myself a mental shake, I focused on her words. Her skin was soft under my hands, but her eyes were distant.

"When was it?" I asked when she paused.

"Just a couple of days ago. Wednesday, maybe?" She rubbed at her temples like she was getting a headache and I didn't blame her. "I was ready to just go home, call it quits." She sighed. "I've been thinking more and more about just quitting."

The expression on her face was near desperate, and I hated it. Hated all of the reasons why she was wearing it.

"I've always wanted to be a prosecutor. Taking some of the monsters off the streets, keeping them off so they can't hurt the innocent." She laughed then and it was an ugly, bitter sound. "But nobody's innocent. Not if you ask Bethany."

"Bethany can get fucked," I said, irritated. I didn't want to talk about Dena's bitch of a boss.

"She does. A lot." Dena looked at me, her eyes turbulent. "Sometimes by mafia hitman."

I stared at her, thinking I had to have misheard her.

"Okay, can you..." I stopped and cleared my throat. "Dena, I think you need to explain that. In detail."

"Are you asking for positions or facts or what?"

"Dena..."

"I saw them, Arik. Bethany was with *that* guy. I went by her office to talk to her – maybe to quit, I don't know – but she was fucking that guy. Or rather, she was being fucked by him. A distinction, I know..."

"The hitman," I said slowly. I had to make sure I was understanding this right. "You're telling me that Bethany McDermott, a Manhattan assistant district attorney, was fucking the guy who pulled a gun on me in my apartment. *That* guy?"

She nodded, clearly distressed.

Easing her off my lap, I got up and started to pace.

Fuck.

What the hell was Bethany thinking?

"That was why I came to the apartment," she said. "To tell you all of this because I have absolutely no clue what to do."

I turned to look at her, but she was staring at the wall. I knew she wasn't seeing it, though. She wasn't seeing anything at that moment, unless it was Bethany and the giant shit-storm her boss had caught her in – not to mention the danger.

"My boss is sleeping with the *mafia*, Arik." She made an amused sound. "And to think I was worried about the ethics of sleeping with a defense attorney."

TWENTY

DENA

"What exactly do you think you're going to find?" Arik asked.

I stood in the middle of my office, arms folded around my middle as I looked around. Shooting him a look over my shoulder, I shook my head. "I don't know."

Coming down here had been a spur of the moment idea, but now that I was here, I had no idea what to do. At least it was Saturday afternoon, which meant the place was essentially deserted. There were a few lingering paralegals and ADAs working on cases, but not enough that Arik and I really needed to worry.

I knew what I needed. Proof that Bethany had ties to the Russian mafia. Something other than the fact that I'd seen her having sex with one of their known hitmen, but beyond that? If I was going to be believed, there would need to be corroboration.

Except I wasn't sure where to start or what even to look for. I also wasn't sure who I could trust.

I sniffed, my nose starting to tingle in a familiar way. Out of habit, I glanced over to see if somebody had brought in more damn flowers, but the table by the door was empty. I rubbed at my nose, annoyed, but turned my thoughts back to the problem at hand.

I had half a mind to call one of the senior partners from my old firm. Granted, it was full of divorce lawyers, but they had connections. One of them was bound to know somebody I could trust, but first I had to find evidence.

Fuck it. There was a reason I hadn't gone into police work.

As if sensing my dilemma, Arik came up behind me and rested his hand on my shoulder. His mouth opened to say something, but before he could manage, a sneeze caught me off guard. Embarrassed, I moved away and went to the desk to dig through my purse. I didn't even have a chance to find tissues before I sneezed a second, then a third time.

"Bless you." He almost sounded amused.

As I turned to rummage for a tissue, Arik chuckled behind me. "Don't tell me you went and developed an allergy to me."

I might have laughed, except my eyes landed on a small vase of flowers sitting discreetly by the window.

"Oh, for crying out loud."

I went over to grab the flowers, but another sneezing fit hit. My right hand hit the vase and it fell, glancing off the corner of the desk and shattering. Water sprayed, and if I hadn't been busy sneezing my head off, I would have started cussing my random flower bringer to hell and back.

As it was, since I *was* busy sneezing, I wasn't the one to see it.

Arik was.

I only heard a door open, close...then his hand squeezed my shoulder. Something about that gesture communicated tension rather than comfort, and as my sneezing eased, I shot him a look. He had one finger pressed to his lips. His face was serious, but when he spoke, his tone was light.

"Well, I guess I'll save a fortune on flowers, won't I?"

His eyes slid down. Once, twice.

Mystified, I didn't say anything, but rather glanced down and saw his hand. He held it out, palm up. There was something inside it. Was that...?

Oh *shit*.

Again, Arik pressed his finger to his lips. Casually, he said, "I dumped the flowers in the trash across the hall. Why don't we step outside, let you breathe some fresh air?"

My entire body was tense, and I was full of questions, but I had to assume the device – the bug – Arik had in his hand was still transmitting to something, somewhere. He dumped the bug into the trash in my office, along with the remains of the vase, and led me into the hallway, his hand on my back.

Once we were out in the hall, I started to walk faster, needing to be away. Arik followed. I didn't have a conscious destination in mind, but a few minutes later, I stood in front of Bethany's office.

Logically, there was no reason why I'd stopped there. It wasn't like she was here. The one thing I did know was that if Bethany was in bed with the mob – insinuation definitely intended – they wouldn't need to bug her office, so if there was any place in the whole building that wouldn't be compromised, it would be here.

I tried to open her door, but of course, it was locked.

As I started to turn away, though, Arik crowded up against me, his voice casual as he said, "I don't think she's going to be in, but it can't hurt to..."

He spoke in a voice louder than necessary for our proximity, and I shot a look up at him. He stood too close for such a public place, and I went to step away, but he caught my arm.

That was when I saw he was busy with his right hand. His body blocked most of his actions, and he tugged me in to hide what he was doing.

"Son of a bitch," I whispered, shocked and furious at the same time. What the hell was he thinking?

Apparently, he was thinking that he knew what he was doing. In under five seconds, he had the door open.

"What do you know, the boss must be in." He gave me a brilliant smile and turned his head as he caught my arm and pulled me into Bethany's empty office.

"You crazy son of a bitch," I said to his back as he locked the door behind him.

He looked at me, a cagey grin on his face. It was so far removed from anything else I'd ever seen from him that it caught me off-guard.

"Two questions — one, how did you learn how to jimmy locks? Two, are you planning on defending us both when we get caught?" I demanded.

"I have absolutely no idea what you are talking about, Ms. Monroe." Arik looked at me, his face the picture of innocence.

For a brief moment, I caught a glimpse of what he must've looked like as a child, getting caught with his hand in the cookie jar. I felt safe in assuming that he'd gotten away with a lot, and not just because he came from a rich family.

His grin softened. "The door was open. We came inside, hoping Bethany might be in, and now we're sitting down, patiently waiting since we assumed she wouldn't leave her door unlocked."

Whatever he'd used to pick the lock had disappeared back wherever it came from in the first place.

Growling, I turned to storm back out into the hall, but then stopped, remembering the reason I'd come here in the first place.

"We are so fucked," I whispered, lifting my face to the ceiling.

Sooner or later, Bethany was going to go down, and because

I was one of her ADAs, I would be guilty by association. My career would be over.

"We're going to be fine." His voice was surprisingly gentle. "Bethany is messing with people's lives, Dena. She's not just screwing with the justice system – and that pisses me off probably as much as it does you – but she's putting people's lives at risk."

I turned toward him and he came to me then, lifting a hand to cradle my cheek. I couldn't stop myself from leaning into the touch.

"Are you willing to take some chances and stop her?"

"Hey, I came to your place yesterday, didn't I? And I didn't freak out with the breaking and entering. Not too much, anyway." With a rueful grin, I stepped away and stared at my boss' office. "So...where do we start? I don't think we're going to find a neatly organized calendar itemized with things like... *screwing the hitman on Wednesday...destroying an innocent woman's life on Thursday...*"

Not even fifteen minutes had passed when a noise came from the hallway.

Panicked, I shot a look to Arik and he grabbed my arm, hauling me to the chairs. "Remember," he said, his voice low as he slowly unlocked the door. "The door was open. And it was for you, so you're not lying. That's all you need to focus on. You came looking for Bethany. Just keep your head and we'll get through this. I promise."

The door swung open, hot and cold chills dancing all over me and I squeezed my eyes, battling back the most intense wave of nausea I'd felt since my first day in court. When I looked at the door, prepared to see Bethany, all the adrenaline drained out in a wave that left me feeling even sicker.

It wasn't her.

"Pierce." I stared at the man in the doorway with a mix of shock and relief. Next to me, I felt Arik relax as well.

Head cocked slightly, the other man studied us silently for a moment before stepping into the room. I opened my mouth to say something, but Arik laid a hand on my arm and gave it a gentle squeeze.

Pierce turned toward the door but instead of shutting it, he nodded and curiosity overrode everything else I was feeling. An older, slightly stooped gentlemen walked in. The man gave both Arik and me a long hard study as Pierce closed the door.

What the hell was going on here?

"The coffee shop across the street would have worked just as well if you needed air," the old man said.

His eyes, sharp and dark, glinted against smooth brown skin. If it wasn't for the pure white hair on his head, and the slight stoop to his shoulders, he could have passed for a much younger man. He came toward me, moving slowly and flicked a glance at Arik.

Without even needing to look at each other, we both stood. I didn't know about him, but I wasn't feeling comfortable dealing with what was going on from a sitting position.

"You." The older man pointed at me. "You have been a pain in the ass from day one, Ms. Monroe."

I blinked, unsure if it was an insult or if I should take it as an unintended compliment.

From the corner of my eye, I saw Pierce opening a glass-fronted cabinet, but I didn't turn to look at him.

"Just how have I been a pain...?" The rest of the question died as Pierce came back to join us.

"We need to leave," he said to the older man. "She's left her apartment. I'm not sure if she's going to come in today or not, but she's made some calls."

Before I could speculate on whatever the hell this meant,

the older man gestured to a door. "We really should talk, Ms. Monroe. I assure you, you'll be interested in what I have to tell you, and I believe you'll want to hear it too. But this isn't the ideal place."

"Are you suggesting a coffee shop?" Arik asked, his voice biting.

"If you wish."

SITTING on a bench in Central Park, I sipped at my coffee while Pierce took his turn talking. The other man looked like he was more caught up in the antics of the kids playing by the Balto statue, but I wasn't fooled.

His name was Washington Rule. He was with the state attorney general's office and apparently, they'd been investigating Bethany for a while now. And Pierce was their inside man. When they'd caught wind of the job opening, they'd pulled some strings to get Pierce in as well.

Washington had also told me he had a feeling his office wasn't the only one looking into her, and if I was as smart as he thought, I'd listen to him, because he would go to bat for me when things went down. Not *if* but *when*. I didn't want to be implicated in her fuck-ups – his words exactly. And he was right about that.

Once Pierce stopped talking, I looked at him. It might've been a bit juvenile, but I had to know. "Is it standard practice to sleep with people you're investigating?"

He smirked at me, lifting his coffee to his lips, but he didn't answer. Apparently, his smug attitude wasn't just a cover. He looked over at Washington, one eyebrow cocked as if to ask, *Shall I answer or do you want this one?*

Washington sighed deeply, leaning forward slightly and pressing the tips of steepled hands to his lips.

"Ms. Monroe. Let me say that we've tried any number of times to get close to Ms. McDermott, and she always manages to keep her cards close to her chest, so to speak. We've tried dozens of times, and she always manages to keep one step ahead of us. So when we had the opportunity to put somebody in her office, and she started to...well..." Washington slid his gaze toward Pierce. "It wasn't exactly what we would have wanted, but I can't say it caught any of us off guard, either. As I said, we've been watching her for some time."

The lawyer in me had to ask. "And what are you going to do when she brings up their relationship in court?"

"It won't be brought up." Pierce shrugged and looked away, whether it was embarrassment or just boredom, I didn't know. "Chances are, Bethany won't ever go to court."

I stiffened, immediately understanding what he meant. "Are you telling me that she's jerking people around, abusing her office and you're going to make a deal with her?"

Washington's eyes narrowed, but it was more speculative than aggressive. "That's the way the system works, Miss Monroe. You use the smaller fish to get to the bigger ones. With the evidence we have on her now, she's not going to risk this going to court, because she's not going to risk her acquaintances thinking she's going to balk on the stand. As soon as she's arrested, they'll be worrying she might become a liability. Once we lay all our cards on the table, she'll be begging for protective custody in the most secure facility we have. And that's assuming we can bring charges before any other agency can. Believe me when I say that her liaisons with Mr. Lawton are nothing you need to concern yourself with."

Rising, I moved over to the edge of the path, staring at the playing children who had so captured Washington's interest a few moments earlier. Arms crossed over my middle, I blew out a breath. Arik had been quiet through all of this, but I'd gotten the impression it was because he was letting me take the lead since it was my boss we were discussing. He was definitely interested in what we were saying.

"Why are you telling me all of this?" I asked finally. "It seems to me that your investigation is going fine the way it is. Why come to me?"

There was a terse moment of silence, followed by a single name.

"Leayna Mance."

Surprised, I looked back at Washington.

"What about her?" That came from Arik. He'd been mostly silent through all of this, but now, as he rose from the bench, I turned to look at him. His jaw was tight and his eyes hard.

Washington looked at me rather than Arik even as he answered the question, "The death of Mr. Mance and the arrest of his wife piqued our interest as we'd been aware of him as something of a player in the Russian mob."

"So you decided to use the case as a way to see where Bethany's loyalties lay?"

"You are quite intelligent, Miss Monroe. I'm sure you would've figured the entire thing out, given a bit more time." He rose and came toward me. "I've had a man going in and out of her office for months, listening, doing odd jobs for her."

It hit me then. "Planting bugs?" I asked.

Washington nodded. "Yes. The flowers were part of the investigation."

"You bugged her office." Arik sounded as pissed as I felt.

"I did." Washington lifted his chin. "I also had my man warn her, as best he could."

Shit. I suddenly realized who the other inside man had

been. Someone who Bethany could order around, but also not see if she didn't need something.

"The janitor. He's the one planting the bugs. He moved everything into my new office." I frowned. "You call that trying to warn me? Could he have been more cryptic?"

"We do what we can." Washington shrugged. "I also had him make some minor adjustments on your phone line, ones that conflicted with the adjustments her people had already made. Since you made most of your calls on your cellphone, she didn't get suspicious when she wasn't getting much from your office line."

As much as I loathed the idea that the state attorney's office had been listening to my calls, I also understood that having Bethany listening would've been much worse. "Thank you."

"I don't want thanks." Washington's voice was hard, but not harsh. "I want you to do your job. You seem to care about justice, truth, making sure the right person pays for the crime."

"I do," I said, wondering where he was going with this.

"Good." His expression hardened. "Because I have work for you to do."

TWENTY-ONE

DENA

Nerves jittered inside me as I waited in the outer office for Eugene Hurst.

The DA.

Bethany's boss. And, technically, my boss too.

Washington had assured me that Mr. Hurst was a good, solid district attorney, and he was the person I needed to speak with. I had a stack of evidence, both what I'd figured out and what Washington and Pierce had collected, and I needed Mr. Hurst to see it before Leayna Mance went to court this afternoon.

When I'd asked Washington why he hadn't just taken things to Mr. Hurst himself, he'd told me that his office was trying to keep things quiet. He knew if he made an appointment to see the DA, word would get back to Bethany and she would know that someone was on to her. If I went, however, it would just look like a newbie ADA trying to kiss up to the boss.

I was just worried that Mr. Hurst wouldn't believe me. I'd been assured that Washington's sources would be in touch with Mr. Hurst shortly to confirm everything I was saying, but I was the one who needed to convince the DA that one of his office's attorneys was operating with some pretty shady personnel and it was imperative that he intervene.

We could've gone to the judge in Leayna's trial to try to get Bethany's motions thrown out, or even delayed, but Washington had informed us that things ran deeper than just Bethany. He had evidence to support that even the judge was involved with the mafia.

So we needed a power player.

Not too many had more power than Hurst when it came to legal hardball. His trial record was among the most impressive in the country, and he'd never been afraid to take on anyone, regardless of who they were. We needed him to handle Leayna's case, as well as making sure Bethany didn't suspect anything. We also needed someone to support Arik's protection request for Leayna.

My stomach had been a mess all weekend, and not even the call from Officer Dunne yesterday saying that the mysterious call I'd received on Friday had been a hoax – some teenagers had been paid a hundred bucks to prank me – had been able to make me feel any less anxious. And it wasn't because I suspected it'd been some of Bethany's friends behind the call. I didn't really care about that.

No, the reason for my nausea and insomnia was simple.

Too much depended on me.

The door opened and a tall, thin man appeared. He looked at me, his lips pursed thoughtfully. After a moment, he beckoned to me and I rose, clutching my bag tightly.

My phone rang and I didn't have to look at it to know who it was.

Bethany.

I hadn't called in sick or given her any sort of indication that I wasn't coming in today. Pierce wasn't there either, and I doubted he'd given her reasons either.

Chances were she was getting pissed, but better pissed than suspicious. And I was pretty sure that a pissed Bethany was someone who made mistakes. Mistakes that could only help at this point.

I'd have to answer her soon, but I wanted to introduce myself first. When the phone buzzed again on my way to the doorway, I grimaced.

"No rest for the weary, Ms. Monroe."

I managed a strained smile. "I thought that was the wicked."

He gave me an amused look. "Well, sometimes the wicked get more rest than they let on, the bastards."

I was pretty sure I was going to like this guy.

He stepped aside and let me enter before shutting the door behind me.

When my phone buzzed again, I gave him an apologetic look. "It's my supervisor. I need to let her know I'm running behind. A quick text, if it's okay."

"Of course, of course. Coffee?"

While the Manhattan DA actually got me coffee, I sent a text that was all lies and sunshine.

Problem on my train in the subway. Be there soon as possible.

I had just sent it off when Mr. Hurst put the coffee down at my elbow.

I'd just lifted the coffee to my lips when Bethany responded. I blanched at her foul reply and almost managed to choke and scald myself at the same time. I barely kept from swearing, but I couldn't stop myself from dropping the phone. Mr. Hurst picked it up, and I could tell by his gaze that he'd read the text, although he said nothing, simply put my phone face-down on the table where he'd placed my coffee.

Then he sat down – not behind the monolithic desk – but in the chair next to mine.

"So just what is it that has you...caught up on the subway, Ms. Monroe?"

His tone was no nonsense, but not judgmental. I felt a stab of hope. Maybe he truly was the real deal.

Lowering my coffee, I started to reach for the bag that held all the evidence I'd been asked to give him, but then I paused and turned toward him. "Do you believe that everybody is guilty? That nobody is innocent, and if you have the bad luck to end up in the wrong place at the wrong time, then you just have to pay the piper?"

He didn't look taken aback by the question. On the contrary, he settled more comfortably in his chair and studied me. One finger tapped his lips while his gaze held mine.

I felt like he was dissecting me, the way he watched me, like he was trying to figure out what made me tick. I didn't let myself look away, though. I had the feeling the next few minutes would make or break things. Not only my career, but also the freedom and lives of everyone connected to this thing. I couldn't let them down.

"If that was how I felt, then I wouldn't – or at least I shouldn't – be sitting here in this office. Wouldn't you agree, Ms. Monroe?"

Blowing out a hard, shaking breath, I smiled a real smile. One of the bands constricting my chest fell away. There was still a lot to do, but I felt better about my chances of convincing him.

"I do agree, sir." I reached into the bag at my feet. The phone on the table rang, but I ignored it.

"Is that your supervisor again?" Mr. Hurst asked.

"Yes." I didn't look at the phone, or at him.

"Is there a reason you're dodging her?"

Focusing on the files and the disc in my hands, I nodded slowly. "Yes, sir. I'm afraid there is." Now, I did look at him.

"My supervisor, she tends to think that way. She wants a win, regardless of a defendant's guilt or innocence. It's not about the truth, or justice. That's not the kind of law I want to practice."

He nodded and gestured toward his desk. I put the files down and took a deep breath. He was going to listen, which meant the rest was up to me.

I started with what I'd done myself.

Over the next hour, as my phone rang repeatedly, and the texts began to come almost on the end of each other, Eugene Hurst and I went over the evidence I'd compiled regarding Leayna Mance. Then we went over the data on her husband, the late Mr. Mance and just how deeply in debt he'd been. When I reached the data showing when he'd come out of debt, Mr. Hurst rose to refill our coffees and I paused to rest my voice.

"I take it you presented all of this to Ms. McDermott."

"Yes."

He came back to me and sat down, holding out the coffee. I accepted, but didn't drink. I was already jittery from nerves, plus the caffeine I'd previously consumed.

"What did your boss say when you presented her with all of this?"

"It depended on the information." I tried not to frown. I couldn't let any of this be personal. It had to be all about the facts. "But it pretty much added up to the same thing. I was told to concentrate my efforts elsewhere, or look deeper because there had to be something else that fit our case better." I hesitated for a moment, then gave a specific example. "There was a break-in at Ms. Mance's penthouse, and when I had nothing to report, Ms. McDermott gave me the impression that I should have made something up."

At that, his graying brows shot up. "And you're certain you didn't misunderstand her?"

"Quite sure, sir."

He shook his head as he looked down at everything I'd spread across his desk. "This is to go before a judge today, correct?"

"Yes, sir." My phone went off again and I resisted the urge to throw it against the wall.

His eyes flicked to it and I had the odd feeling *he* wanted to do the same thing. He reached over and picked up his phone.

I listened as he called his administrative assistant in, and over the next five minutes, I sat, an enthralled audience of one as the two of them successfully managed to pull Leayna's case from the docket.

"Reason, sir?" his assistant asked, her eyes competent and focused. She never once looked at me, her attention focused solely on him.

I didn't mind. It was clear it wasn't a slight to me, but rather just her doing her job.

"A last minute change in council." He wasn't looking at her. His eyes skimmed one of the files in front of him. "I'm taking over the case personally, and as I haven't had a chance to review all the evidence, I'll be unable to be there this afternoon." He paused and then looked up at her. "If Judge Engler has a problem with that, have her contact me directly."

"Yes, sir."

He turned to another page, putting the one he'd been reading facedown. "That should be all for now, Ms. Holcomb."

"Yes, sir." She turned to go.

"Oh, if by chance Ms. McDermott calls, I'm indisposed." The look he gave her over the edge of his glasses was hard, the sort of look that had gotten him his reputation as one of the toughest DA's in the country. "I'll be able to talk to her soon, but not today."

Once we were alone, he blew out a breath and looked at

me, a wry expression on his face. "I expect I'll be talking to Bethany McDermott a great deal more than I wish in the days to come."

Unfortunately, I was pretty sure he was right.

"Now that we have that taken care of," he said as he sat down again. "I think it's time to look over the rest of what you have." He glanced at the clock. "I'll have Ms. Holcomb call in lunch. Do you like Indian food?"

BY THE TIME LUNCH ARRIVED, I was pretty sure I wasn't going to work today.

Right after lunch, Mr. Hurst excused himself, and when he came back into the office, he had a look of aggrieved frustration in his eyes that made me almost feel sorry for him.

He'd had a dirty ADA in his house, and he hadn't known. Now he had to clean house, and try to explain how he'd missed it. I had a bad feeling that it wasn't going to stop with Bethany either. If Washington's intel was accurate, a lot of people were going to spend a lot of time in jail.

Sometime around three, Mr. Hurst escorted a couple of men in suits into the room, and I had my first encounter with the FBI who were investigating Bethany. Washington had been right about that.

The two FBI agents subjected me to a rather grueling series of questions about where I'd come up with my information. I supposed they believed they were intimidating me, but considering everything I'd been through over the last few days, I just found it aggravating.

When I explained my source was confidential, they threatened to arrest me. Before I could say a word, Mr. Hurst intervened and handed them their asses. They didn't like me any better after that, but at least they didn't try to threaten me again.

The day was proving to be insightful, frustrating, aggravating, enlightening...and damn long.

At the end of the day, however, Mr. Hurst did give me the news that made all of it worthwhile.

Bethany had been detained just as she tried to leave her office that afternoon. She'd also attempted to have a janitor shred a rather substantial number of documents that had somehow found their way into the hands of the New York City Police Department.

I wasn't a huge fan of Washington or Pierce, considering how that investigation had been run, but I was glad their source had given the information to the local cops rather than the Feds. Granted, it was probably to ensure that it stayed in-house, but after the way the FBI agents had acted toward me, I wasn't feeling particularly friendly toward them.

As Mr. Hurst walked with me to the elevators, he said, "You worked pretty damn hard to help out somebody on the opposite side of the law."

I stopped and looked at him. "It was never about Leayna Mance being accused of murder or me versus her. It was about justice, about making sure an innocent person wasn't sentenced for a crime they didn't commit."

"I like your attitude, Dena." For the first time in several hours, he smiled. "I hope this hasn't soured you on working for this office. I'll be needing to fill some positions soon, I suspect. You're not quite ready to go solo, but I need people like you around here."

He held out his hand.

Slowly, I reached out and took it. "Thank you, sir."

He nodded at me.

As I turned to leave, I saw a cluster of men in suits waiting for the elevators as well. The FBI, come to play. I sighed, then almost tripped over my feet, as my eyes landed on one of them.

"Son of..." I dropped my bag, my fingers suddenly nerveless.

The man I'd seen came up and knelt in front of me. He gave me an easy grin, smiling as he began to gather up the things I'd spilled.

The last time I'd seen him, he'd been bleeding, but those eyes had still been laughing. Laughing as he'd been taken from Arik's apartment in handcuffs.

Adrenaline flooded through me, and I grabbed the first thing that came to hand – my phone. Like I'd be able to do anything with that.

"You look like you've seen a ghost," he said, his voice softer than it had been, but the accent still there. "Ms. Monroe, are you well?"

"Mikel, come on," one of the agents behind him said, his voice hard and flat.

He ignored the man, leaning in. "You broke my nose, Dena. I almost broke my cover over that, you know," he said, whispering directly into my ear. "Good work, by the way."

Broke his cover?

What the hell was going on here? Why were the Feds not dragging him away from me?

Dazed, I watched as he straightened, and when he did, I saw the badge.

Hanging around his neck was a lanyard with the words *FBI* in large, unmistakable font. His picture and the name *Mikel Bobrov.*

But that...that wasn't the name I'd seen with his picture before.

Were they fucking kidding me? Rubbing a hand across my eyes, I shook my head. After all the shit those two agents had given me, they'd never even once thought to tell me that Arik and I hadn't actually been in danger the other day. Or that they had a fucking inside man high enough in the mob to be considered one of the top assassins on the payroll.

I was going to be so fucking glad when this shit was all over.

———————

I'D WANTED to get through the rest of the day without any surprises, but as I walked down the steps and saw the man waiting for me, I thought maybe I could change my mind about that.

Arik had his hands in his pockets, and a smile on his face, which told me that at least he wasn't delivering bad news. I wanted to smile in return, but the entire day – hell, the entire month – had worn on me, and I found I had a hard time smiling or even standing there. I wanted to drop down on the ground and just sit. Sit and stare and not think about anything.

Well, that wasn't entirely true, I amended as I made my way down the steps. If I was going to be honest, what I really wanted was to curl up with Arik, have him naked against me. On top of me. Behind me.

My breath hitched a little as my heart gave an unsteady thump. Maybe what I *really* wanted was something I hadn't had in a long time, but this wasn't really the time and place to tell him that. Especially since I really didn't know how he felt.

"You look like you've had a rougher day than I have," Arik said softly as I took another step toward him.

All around us, the city continued to buzz and rush, but with him standing there, I felt like I could be still for a little while. I felt like I could just...*be*.

"Yeah." With a slow nod, I said, "That sounds about right."

He brushed his fingers across my cheek, a light touch, but

enough to confirm my previous revelation for me.

"What are you thinking about?" he asked, his voice doing that warm caress thing that made me shiver.

I tried not to lean into him, but it was where my body wanted to be. Where I wanted to be. I couldn't tell him that though. Not here, not like this. "I really want to be outside of my head for a while. But..." My voice trailed off.

He finished my thought. "We need to talk."

"Yeah." I forced myself to look away. Talk seemed like such a small word to describe what we needed to do.

"Come on." He took my hand as he raised his other one to hail a cab. Apparently, he hadn't driven in today. We were silent for a minute before he spoke again, "They've dropped the charges."

Whipping my head around, I looked up at him. "Leayna's free?"

"Yeah." He crooked a grin at me, and then lifted his face to the sky, sighing deeply. "She's already packed a few bags, contacted some personal security, and she'll be hightailing it out of the city first thing tomorrow. She's going to stay with some friends out of town, and has promised to contact me as soon as she arrives so if anything happens to her between now and then, I'll know. I don't think it'll be a problem though. I think pretty much all of her new security detail are ex-Marines or Rangers or Seals or something like that."

"Good for her." I meant it. Her freedom wasn't just a reminder that the justice system, however flawed, could still work. I felt glad for her personally. She'd been through a lot and deserved a fresh start.

"Good for us, too."

I looked over at Arik, startled by his statement.

He opened the back door of the cab and stepped aside to let

me get in first. After he'd slid in next to me and closed the door, he gave the cabbie an address, then turned back to me.

"Now that we don't have her case between us, we can finally have a real conversation." His gaze was intense, making me want to squirm. "No more interruptions. No excuses. One way or another, we're going to figure this out."

Shit.

The Waldorf Astoria wasn't exactly the place I would have chosen to take Dena, but we couldn't go to my place in the city – it was still off limits. I wasn't sure if her place was safe yet either, and the club just seemed like a bad idea. We could've gone all the way back to the house, but I wasn't sure I could last that long of a drive without addressing what was unsettled between us. Besides, I had a feeling neutral ground was the way to go.

But I wasn't about to take her to the Holiday Inn.

Judging by the expression in her eyes, she seemed to appreciate the surroundings, even if she didn't say it. As we rode the elevator up to the room, she slid me a look, a nervous little smile on her lips.

I didn't let myself lean over and kiss her.

I wanted to.

It was going to be hard enough to keep my hands off her once we got inside a room that had a bed *right there*, so the last thing I needed to do was start down the road to temptation. And even a chaste kiss with her, an innocent touch, was a temptation. Hell, just looking at her, thinking about her, made me want to...shit. I needed to get my thoughts away from that direction immediately.

With my hands securely in my pockets, I said softly, "I was surprised to hear from the DA's office so quickly."

"Eugene Hurst apparently doesn't waste time."

She stared at the doors, her fingers toying with a charm hanging from her necklace. The necklace itself was a slim silver collar, while the charm was long, thin and black, elegant and simple. I wondered if it was some sort of good luck charm, something with sentimental value. A flash of jealousy went through me at the thought that maybe someone had given it to her. A male someone.

Fuck.

I wanted to see her wearing nothing but that necklace while I wore nothing but her, wrapped around my cock.

Focus.

"I take it he believed you."

She blew out a breath, but before she had a chance to answer, the elevator stopped and the doors silently glided open. I gestured for her to exit and followed her into the hallway. In silence, we moved to our room and I unlocked it, stepping aside so she could enter. After closing the door behind us, I moved through the room, checking it out to ensure it was as secure as I'd hoped it'd be.

Once I'd finished, I turned to find her at the window. She stood with her arms wrapped around her middle, head tipped to the side so that her hair hid her face. I hadn't realized how much longer it'd gotten since I'd first seen her.

The need to gather that hair in my hand, bare her neck, brush my lips across the elegant slope hit me hard. I wanted to kiss her skin, lick my way down, down, down...

Fuck.

I wanted her against me through the night, wrapped in my arms. I wanted to wake up with her in the morning.

I sighed and raked my hands through my hair. "You were right when you said this would be complicated."

She angled her head, smiling a little as our gazes met. "I'm right about a lot of things."

The calm confidence in her voice was just one more thing that got to me. I was shocked at how much I enjoyed seeing her like that, enjoyed knowing how strong she was...and how it felt when someone that strong submitted.

Still, there were things we needed to discuss.

"Has all this soured things for you at the DA's office?"

Dena took a slow, steadying breath and turned to face me fully, leaning back so that her hips were braced against the windowsill. With the city as a backdrop, she studied me, and I waited, knowing she'd answer when she was ready.

"I thought it might," she said after a minute. "But Bethany wasn't a real lawyer. I can't let her be the filter through which I base my choices. Besides, I spent more than half my life wanting to be a lawyer, wanting to put the bad guys away so they couldn't hurt people. What would it say about me if I let the first real bad guy I came across be the one to take that dream away?"

I crossed over to her.

Her eyes swept toward mine, and her breath caught as I brushed her hair back. Her lips parted, her tongue sliding out to dampen her lips.

Shit. I had no idea how I was going to have this conversation if she kept doing things like that.

"What made you want to be a lawyer?" I asked suddenly. "A prosecutor?"

She bit her lower lip and her gaze slid away. But not before I'd seen the shadow on her face, in her eyes.

"When I was four, the girl who used to baby-sit me disappeared suddenly. It wasn't until I was twelve that I found out what had happened. Jenny was married to this guy who used to beat her. One day, he went too far. Killed her."

Fuck.

"He got off on a technicality though," she continued. "Went away for a couple years. Then he came back and married the older sister of one of my classmates. He killed her six months later. Beat her to death, the same as Jenny. Manslaughter. Six to ten."

Pushing a hand into her hair, I tangled my fingers in the soft strands. "I'm so sorry."

"What about you?" she asked. "What got you into this?"

I gave her a sad smile. "Actually, my story's not too different from yours. Just from the other side."

She looked up at me, puzzled.

I didn't like telling this story, but she'd told me hers.

"The house I took you to, it was my uncle's. When I was a kid, he was arrested. His wife was found dead in a hotel, and the cops arrested him. It couldn't have been him, though. He was with us when she died. No one believed us. Said we were his family, of course we'd lie."

Sighing, I dipped my head and pressed my forehead to hers, rubbing my thumb against the soft underside of her chin. She didn't say anything, but I didn't need her to. All I needed was her to be there.

I continued, "The trial, all of it...it was too much. He killed himself, put a bullet in his brain the day before they read the verdict. I don't think he would have been found guilty, but he was tired. Tired of the guilt, the speculation. Tired of missing her and wondering who had really killed her."

Dena reached up and put her hand on my face. "Did anybody ever find out what happened?"

"Not officially." Rubbing my cheek against her palm, I thought back to the side investigation I'd done on my own, years later. "But she'd been involved with somebody. A cop. And when she died, she was pregnant."

"Oh, baby." Dena's expression softened and she pressed a kiss to my lips. "I guess we both went into this for our own reasons."

"Yeah." Looking out the window to the city she'd been staring at, I said softly, "You don't get to pick and choose your cases, Dena. A prosecutor for the city of Manhattan can't."

Something flickered in her eyes, and I knew she was thinking that I was ending things, that it was too much.

Hell, no.

Stroking a finger across the soft curve of her lower lip, I tugged her closer, and told her what I needed to tell her before I chickened out.

"I can. I've talked to the senior partners, and I told them I don't want to take any cases that'll be in Manhattan."

"Arik—"

I kissed her hard and fast, pushing my tongue past her lips. I had to have that one taste, now. Just in case.

She was panting when I pulled back until only a few inches separated our mouths.

"I want this to work," I told her roughly, silently begging her to agree. "We have something. You know it. I know it. I want it to work, but if we're constantly dancing around things because of our jobs, we won't have a chance. Since you don't have any control over the jobs you'll be assigned, then I'll control the clients I'll accept."

Dena closed her eyes and curled her arms around my neck, but she didn't say anything.

Nerves started to pulse inside me. Shit. I was usually a patient person, but I didn't think I could make it much longer.

"You know, you could give me an idea what you're thinking."

"Be quiet a minute," she said, her voice husky.

I was hoping that was a good thing. She hadn't pulled away, and she still didn't as I held her, skimming my hand up and down her spine. I focused on that, on the feel of her, hoping to distract myself.

I tried. I really did. But I couldn't give her that minute. I had to know.

"Dammit, Dena. I just moved here. I'm trying to make senior partner, and I'm making demands on the top guys. You're worth it, but it would be nice to know if I'm doing this for a reason or wasting my..."

Dena's mouth slid against mine. As the chaos in my head tumbled to a halt, she stroked her tongue across my lower lip, scraped her teeth over it. Then she pulled back enough to speak.

"I'm not entirely sure how you ended up in my life, Arik, but I'm damn grateful."

Her words slid over me, through me, settled deep inside me. The relief was enough to make my knees weak.

Gripping her waist even tighter, I pulled her flush against me. I had to hear her say it. "Then we're going to make this happen?"

"Seems to me that we already are." Her mouth pressed to mine, then widened into a smile. When she spoke, her breath was hot against my skin. "You know, we're in this beautiful hotel. It seems that we should take advantage of it."

I liked the sound of that.

"Yeah. We should."

TWENTY-THREE

DENA

The feel of his hands on me was every bit as erotic as it had been that first night. The impact of his eyes just as cutting, just as deep.

Now, standing in front of the window, with him behind me, we stared at our wavy reflections, my breath hitching as he freed one button, then another and another.

The city spilled out before us in a glittery array of lights just beyond the darkness of Central Park. I'd always loved the city at night, and tonight was no different.

Except it wasn't just the city we were looking at.

He stripped my shirt away, then caught my wrists. "Put your hands on the window."

I did, the glass cool against my palms, while the heat of Arik – the heat of *need* pulsed everywhere else – inside me, around me, behind me as he leaned down and pressed a kiss to the nape of my neck.

The catch on my bra gave, and I started to lower my hands so he could remove it. I wanted to feel his hands on me so badly that my skin nearly ached.

"Don't move," he said.

I froze, my body humming with anticipation.

The straps on my shoulders loosened. Man, multi-way bras...such a blessing, and I hadn't even considered this one.

I felt bereft when he stopped touching me to neatly fold the bra and put it off to the side. He seemed to take his time before he put his hands back on me again. My nipples throbbed and pulsed, hard little points. The need to have him touching me there was almost too much. When he put his hands on my waist, I arched my spine, instinctively readying myself to push my breasts into his hands.

But when he did touch me, it was to reach for the zipper of my skirt, dragging it down with excruciating slowness. Damn him.

"The bad thing about being here instead of at my place or the club, I have to improvise. No cuffs, no crop." His fingers tripped up my spine, a teasing sensation that left me shivering. "I don't want you moving, so you'll have to restrain yourself. You can't move until I tell you."

Flexing my hands against the windows, I dropped my head. "And what if I do?"

Arik brought his hand down on my ass with a sharp crack. "I just might not fuck you."

Keening low in my throat, I bit my inner cheek. I didn't think he'd actually do it. Or rather, not do it. His need was as obvious as my own. But I could never tell with him. He might choose to spend the rest of the night teasing me.

"That got your attention, didn't it?"

"Bastard." Squeezing my eyes closed, I reached deep inside for all the control I could muster. Fortunately, I had a decent amount.

He spanked me again, the heat spreading across my skin. "Call me names and maybe I won't fuck you anyway. Maybe I'll just get myself off, leave you...wanting."

Groaning, I tucked my head against the crook of my arm. "Arik, please..."

"Say you're sorry. Maybe I'll forgive you, Dena." Despite his words, his tone was gently teasing.

"I'm sorry," I said immediately.

"Want to make it up to me?" His voice dropped.

"Yes." What I actually wanted was to feel him inside me, and these hot, crazy games were almost more than I could handle tonight.

He skimmed a finger along the crevice of my ass. "Just how far are you willing to go to make it up to me, Dena?"

Anything. Just as long as he'd fuck me. "Whatever you want."

When he stopped touching me, my knees started to quake but that was nothing compared to what happened when he buried his hand in my hair, pulling me away from the mirror, forcing my body upright.

"I'm going to tell you something, Dena...I lied. I'm not entirely unprepared."

He kept me like that, one hand in my hair while the other reached down between us.

When I felt the lube-slicked finger probing between the cheeks of my ass, the air I had in my lungs came out in a rush.

Oh, fuck.

He bit my ear, and then said, "I'm going to fuck your ass, good and hard. You're going to moan. You're going to scream. You're going to come. And later, if you're a good girl, I'll clean you up and fuck you again."

I gasped as he pushed two fingers inside me at once. My legs shook as pain and pleasure coursed through me. My clit throbbed even as he worked his fingers deeper.

There was a hard edge to Arik's hunger tonight, a deep, insatiable sort of need, and it washed over me, battering at me like waves against the beach. When he spread his fingers inside me and then twisted, I whimpered, arching a little as I fought to accommodate the penetration that would prepare me for an even deeper one. Usually, I would've wanted him to start with one, then work his way up to two, but another part of me wanted it like this.

The ache spread, my clitoris pulsing and I lowered my hand, needing to relieve the tension.

Arik bit my shoulder, hard enough to draw my attention momentarily. "Don't," he warned.

I whimpered. "Arik, please..."

He spanked me this time, hard, and without his steadying hand at my hip, I twisted on the fingers that invaded me.

"Be still and don't move, or I won't fuck this sweet ass, Dena."

I didn't prefer anal sex, but there were times when I wanted the intensity of it. Right now, I needed him inside me, and I didn't particularly care where.

Curling my hands into fists, I braced myself on the window, and told myself not to move again. I even managed to keep that promise, right up until he removed his fingers and started to work his dick into me instead.

Despite his preparations, it wasn't easy. My ass burned as he kept up the slow, steady pressure, forcing himself inside. I rose up on my toes this time, twisting my spine although I don't know if I was trying to take him deeper or if I was trying to escape.

Arik went still. "Do you want me to stop?"

I shook my head, my breathing harsh. "No. Please, please...please don't, Arik."

He smoothed one hand over the slight curve of my hip. "Convince me. Tell me what you want me to do, Dena."

"I want you to fuck me, Arik." Heat sizzled and burned

through me even as some part of me wondered at how easily he drew submission from me. "I want to feel your cock in my ass."

He put his mouth against my ear. "Are you going to be still for me?"

Whimpering, I whispered, "I'm going to try."

Inside me, he pulsed and I was excruciatingly aware of every inch of him, both what was inside, and what was still to come.

"You better try very hard, baby."

Then he began to move again, slow, pushing his cock into me in increments that seemed to take forever. My entire body was quivering, shaking. It was pure torture. Then, just when I thought he was almost ready to stop the torment, he would withdraw, and I had to bite my lip to keep from screaming.

But this was what I wanted. Why I wanted him. I knew I could give myself to him and he'd not only take it, he'd give me what I needed. He'd protect me.

When he was finally completely seated inside me, a harsh, shuddering moan escaped my throat, and I would have sagged if he hadn't steadied me with an arm around my waist. He rolled his hips, withdrawing just enough to have me tensing up, and then he filled me again.

"I love taking you like this," he said against my ear. "You grab at my dick and you squeeze it so tight...it's like you can't decide if you love it or not. Tell me, Dena. Do you love it?"

"Yes." Forgetting yet again that he didn't want me moving, I reached up and caught the back of his neck. "I love it...I love you, Arik."

He went rigid and I froze. I hadn't meant to say it like that, but it was the truth. A moment later, he pulled out of me altogether, and I sucked in a breath. One that carried pain, shock and disappointment.

He spun me around to face him, one hand coming up to cup my chin.

"What?" he demanded.

"I..." Blinking, a little dazed, I stared at him. I didn't understand what was happening.

He kissed me roughly, his teeth sinking into my lower lip. "What did you say?"

Oh, that.

"I..." Breath coming raggedly now, I met his eyes as he looked at me.

Shit. I'd never said those words to a guy. I'd never met anyone who I'd wanted to say those words to before. I'd come close, but what I'd felt on those few occasions was nothing like what I felt for him.

I might've been terrified, but I wasn't a coward.

"I said I love you."

"Dena..."

He kissed me again, and this time, it was soft and sweet.

My head was spinning when he picked me up, and then it seemed like the whole world was as he carried me into the bathroom.

"What..." The question was smothered under another kiss, and when he broke away, he was setting me on my feet, the tile cold under my soles.

The bathroom was gorgeous, large enough that half my living room could have fit in here and the sunken tub made me want to climb inside it and lounge around for maybe a week.

"What are we doing in here?" I asked, completely confused.

"I'm going to shower. You are too."

His voice had an odd note to it. Feeling a little off balance, I stared up at him. "Um...why?"

He backed me up to the clear glass wall that separated the

shower from the rest of the bathroom.

"Because," he said, kissing me again. Another soft, slow kiss, one that smoldered rather than exploded. "I'm going to make love to you. In that bed. Where I can see your face, and then you're going to say those words to me again. I'm going to have that soft, sweet pussy wrapped around me when you say it. That means...we have to shower."

"Oh." I couldn't manage anything else.

Dazed now, I let him guide me into the shower, let him nudge me under the water. It criss-crossed out from all corners, pounding at my body and hitting muscles that were so tense, I'd forgotten just *how* tense they were. How this whole thing had stretched me thin and tight.

Arik had shown me any number of faces: the sharp lawyer, the wicked lover, the playful lock-pick, the sinful, sexy seducer.

But now he was showing me another side, a side that seemed almost...unsettled, by what I said. But he hadn't run away, hadn't told me that he didn't feel the same way. Instead, he washed me, dried me, and I was little more than putty when he scooped me up into his arms and carried me out of the bathroom. He'd dried me in the stall, murmuring in my ear that he didn't want me getting cold.

I couldn't even fathom being cold, not now. With the downy softness of the mattress under me and the hard, hot length of him above me, the only thing I could *really* fathom was him.

He pressed kiss after kiss to my mouth, my neck, my breasts.

Every time I tried to draw him down to me, he'd come, but only for a moment, only until a series of teasing kisses had my hands limp and lax against his shoulder, and I forgot how to do anything more complicated than breathing and moaning.

Then he caught my hands and pinned them above my head. His eyes locked with mine as he settled between my legs.

"Tell me again, Dena," he said against my lips as he thrust

inside me.

I cried out, arching up against him. My climax was so close, it was almost painful. I stared up at him, my hips rising to meet his. It was as though nothing else existed.

Just him. Just me. Just us.

"Tell me," he ordered.

I couldn't deny him. "I love you."

He caught me in his arms and rolled, shifting our positions. I moaned as it drove him deeper, higher inside me. Hands braced on his chest, I let my head fall back as I rolled my hips against his. Fuck, that felt good.

"Arik..."

"Look at me." His hands tightened on my hips, and the command in his voice managed to cut through the fog in my head.

Forcing my lashes up, I met his eyes. He looked up at me, the vivid emerald color of his gaze searing me.

"I love you, Dena."

The climax slammed into me, hitting me with almost as much force as his words.

Almost.

But not quite.

"Say it again."

TWENTY-FOUR

DENA

"You look beautiful."

Looking into the mirror, I saw Arik standing in the doorway and grinned at him. "You better close the door. Seriously, Arik. Gavin was teasing Carrie about how he wasn't going to wait until the ceremony before he saw her today, and she's panicking because she thinks he meant it."

It was the middle of June, and in just over an hour, Carrie would be marrying Gavin.

I had a feeling Gavin's teasing had been meant as a distraction so she wouldn't panic about all the small, inconsequential details. Except, now she was panicking over her soon-to-be-husband jinxing their wedding by catching a look of her in her wedding dress before the ceremony.

Krissy was going to beat the shit out of him. Sometimes men were just clueless.

Arik slid inside and shut the door behind him. He came to me and bent down, just barely grazing my lips with a kiss before straightening up and looking around. His eyes landed on Krissy and DeVon. He smiled at me.

"Seems like I'm not the only one who couldn't wait to see his woman."

There was a bit of sadness to that smile, and we both knew why. It was the same reason why DeVon was in here, and it wasn't simply because he couldn't bear to be away from her.

He wasn't exactly hovering over her – Krissy would never allow that – but he was staying close. My heart ached more than a little for them both.

"How is she?" Arik moved in closer and pitched his voice low so no one else could hear.

Looking up at him, I shrugged and managed a smile. "I couldn't say. I've never been where she is. She seems to be holding it together pretty well. Losing the baby..."

I swallowed and turned back to the mirror, staring hard at my reflection. If I thought too hard about it, I'd get teary and if I cried today, I'd rather it be over happy things. Happy.

"You know," Arik said as he put his hand on my shoulder. "I've been thinking."

"Today is *not* a day for thinking." Slanting a look up at him, I made a face before leaning forward to study my reflection. I was still wearing my robe, but my make-up and hair were done. Those were the two big things. The dress was the easy thing, for me at least. Carrie had gone with a simple, strapless style that flattered all of us.

Carrie's dress, however, wasn't simple. She had a designer confection that would take several people to help her get into.

If I ever got married, I think I wanted to do a beach wedding. Something where I could wear a simple little white dress and no shoes. Well, considering the height difference, maybe shoes wouldn't be a bad idea, at least for the ceremony...

"Regardless, I *have* been thinking—"

The door swung open and a harried looking guy in a bad

suit came in. His eyes narrowed when he saw Arik and DeVon.

"You two. *Out.* We want some shots of the bridal party getting ready and you two can't be in here for those."

Arik open his mouth to say something, but I leaned in, caught his hand. "This is what Carrie wants. Please, baby."

He blew out a breath, then nodded. Before he turned, he added, "We still need to talk."

"It can wait." Rolling my eyes at his back, I focused on the mirror once more. Pictures of the bridal party getting ready. "What is the deal with that anyway?" I muttered. "We sit around powdering our noses?"

A few feet away, Krissy laughed and the sound made my heart lighten. "Sure. Powder our noses, give each other manicures, maybe have a pillow fight."

I shot her a look and she rolled her eyes. "I think this is something they like doing, coming in hoping we're half-naked."

"Oh, please."

IT TOOK Arik nearly an hour to fight his way back inside. And fight was pretty close to the right word.

There was a woman at the door, one of Carrie's relatives. She'd planted her statuesque frame there, and was practically doing background checks before she let anybody in once the photographers left.

Even they tried to come back in, but Carrie sent them away, saying she'd rather hold off on the rest of the pictures until she actually *looked* like a bride.

I'd had to laugh at that.

Now, though...well, she looked like a bride and I found myself getting a little sniffly. At least this time, it was for a good reason.

Carrie didn't seem to be getting overly emotional just yet, and she proved it by shouting out, "Aunt Ida, it's Dena's date you're arguing with. He can come back if he wants. I don't think it's considered bad luck for *him* to see me. I doubt he's got Gavin hiding in his suit." Then she muttered under her breath, "Though I wouldn't put it past the bastard to try."

Krissy, Leslie and I shared a grin.

Carrie rolled her eyes at us in the mirror and went back to sitting like a statue as the hairdresser did last minute fixes on her already perfect hair.

"It's a good thing we go out there in the next few minutes," Leslie said, rolling her eyes. "That woman might try to flat-iron and twist her hair out of existence if we stayed back here much longer."

"That's why I advocate short hair," I responded to her, but my attention was on Arik as he cut around flowers and everything else in the room.

He came to a stop in front of me, halting maybe five feet away. "I know it's supposed to be the bride's day, but I think the most beautiful woman is standing in front of me."

"I heard that!" Carrie called out, branding an eyelash curler.

"Technically, Carrie, all of you are standing in front of me," Arik replied without taking his eyes off of me.

"Don't be a lawyer today." Carrie made a harrumphing sound under her breath, but I heard the smile.

"Her mother will be rushing us out soon," I told him, gesturing to the dry-erase board that had the schedule written out on it.

Carrie's mom was like a drill sergeant. I was slightly in awe...and a little scared. I was pretty sure Gavin felt the same way.

"That's fine." He held out a hand. "Five minutes."

"What's the hurry?" As he folded his fingers around mine,

I let him guide me to the corner, but when he would have kissed me, I turned away. "I don't believe in kiss-proof lipstick, pal."

"You're cruel. Cruel, evil and malicious," he said with a sigh.

"Guilty as charged." Reaching up, I traced my fingers over his lips. "I'll make it up to you...later. I promise."

"Good." He closed his hand over my wrist and squeezed gently. "Listen...I need to do this now. I kept telling myself I'd wait, but I was talking to DeVon, and seeing Krissy...I can't quit thinking about it."

My stomach lurched.

What was he...?

Arik shoved his hands in his pockets. "I know we haven't even been together a year. I know that. But after everything that's happened and after how Krissy and DeVon lost the baby... I just...look, I don't want to wait forever to start living my life with you."

Mystified, I stared at him. "Arik, we're already—"

"No." He closed the distance between us and stooped down until we were eye to eye. Thanks to my heels, that wasn't as much distance as usual. "We're dating, yes. I sleep at your place on the weekends, or you stay at mine. But sometimes, especially when we're with a busy case, we can go almost a week without seeing each other. It's too long. I want a life with you. A real one."

He nodded toward the women standing beyond us, at Krissy and Carrie and how they stood together laughing. "I want what they have. Something permanent—something real. Maybe later on, a family, if that's what you want, too. I just...I want more than the semi-casual thing we're doing. I want forever, Dena."

Feeling a little weak in the knees, I struggled to breathe as he leaned in and took my hand, lifting it to his lips.

"I want you to move in with me."

His words tumbled over and over in my head as he kissed the back of my hand. He wanted us to live together. I'd never lived with anyone but a college roommate. I'd never lived with a man.

"What do you think?" Arik asked.

I said the first thing that came to mind.

"No."

Arik tensed.

"What?"

The word was flat, and I hurried to clarify.

"I don't mean *no*. Not exactly." Frowning and feeling stupid, I rubbed my forehead. "It's just, I don't really feel like I'm home when I'm at your place. It's gorgeous, and huge, and expensive, but the only thing there I like is you. I don't want to give up my place, even if it is smaller."

His eyes met mine and I saw the hope in them. Hope that I wasn't actually turning him down.

"I want you to move in with me."

Arik stared at me for a moment and then he started to smile.

"Why, Ms. Monroe, you drive a hard bargain. Anybody ever tell you that you like to throw your weight around a bit too much?"

"Well..." I lifted a shoulder. "I just know what I want."

A wolfish grin lit his face. "I've always admired that in a woman." He caught me against him and before I could remember to tell him *not* to, he kissed me, hard, fast and deep. I was panting when he stopped, and ready to beg for more.

"I think I can agree to those terms...as long as I still get to be in charge in the bedroom."

"I can agree to those terms." I arched my eyebrow. "Most of the time."

He tugged me close again, but he didn't have a chance to do anything else.

The door opened and Mrs. Summers stood there, beaming at us. "It's time!" Her soft, southern drawl was warm and sweet – and brooked no argument.

Arik offered me his arm. "Allow me to escort you, Miss Monroe."

"I'd be honored, Mr. Porter." I wrapped my arm around his.

As we started out of the room, he bent his head close to my ear and murmured, "After this, I think we should go back to your – our place – tonight. Make it official. I'll make love to you in every room. What do you think?"

What did I think?

Hmmm...where would I start?

My face was flushed as we walked by the beaming mother of the bride.

"I like the sound of that."

THE END
Club Prive continues in *A Legal Affair (Club Prive Book 9)*, available now. Turn the page for a free preview.

LEGAL AFFAIR PREVIEW

ONE
LESLIE

Eying the clock, I tried not to think about everything I needed to do between now and the time I could leave.

Maybe I didn't punch in and out, but I did have to work so many hours in order to bill my clients, and since Calvin and Associates didn't actually have any associates, I did a hell of a lot of overtime.

I needed another me.

Actually, I needed another lawyer or at the very least, a paralegal.

I had an administrative assistant, and Haley was amazing, but I needed help with more than just administrative tasks. I needed a paralegal and a lot more than the intern I got on a limited basis too.

I'd been trying to find help for a while, but so far, no dice.

The past couple of weeks had been crazy, but most of that was because I'd been trying to juggle a personal life on top of business more than normal.

My heart gave a girly sigh as I remembered the wedding I attended not that long ago.

Carrie and Gavin were ridiculously perfect together, and so happy.

Seeing Krissy had sent a pang through me, too, though not a good one. She'd seemed like she was holding together okay after her miscarriage, but how was I to know? I'd never wanted kids, couldn't even fathom the idea. Krissy, she'd been walking on cloud nine ever since she'd gotten the positive test result...and then it was just gone. She lost the baby, and she'd gone from cloud nine straight down to the lowest sort of hell.

Although we didn't talk as much as we had when we worked together, I knew how hard it'd been on her.

I missed my friends.

Which was why, in a couple of hours, I was hooking up with my closest friend.

It wouldn't be exactly the same as before, of course. Dena was living with her boyfriend – or rather, *he* was living with *her*. Arik was a defense attorney for the rich and powerful and wasn't *that* a joke. Dena had finally landed her dream job, which was usually working for the people who fought *against* the rich and powerful. The ADA and the defense attorney. It should've been a *Lifetime* movie.

But she was happy.

That meant a lot.

So far, I'd only spent a short amount of time in Arik's presence, but Dena seemed happier than I'd ever seen her, so that was all that mattered as far as I was concerned.

The song on the radio changed and I sighed, feeling more despondent than normal.

The love song rolling out of the surround sound had a knot welling up in my throat, and all I really wanted to do was put down my pen and shut down for the day.

No, what I really wanted to do was curl my knees to my chest and listen to the song, maybe sing along for a bar or two.

As the woman wailed about how love had left her behind, I had to fight not to chime in.

Sing it, sister.

I needed to push this melancholy away before I hooked up with Dena.

Not that long ago, the two of us were the ones who'd meet up and reminisce over the good old days, when it had been the four of us – Carrie, Krissy, Dena and me – hitting the town and looking to raise hell and have as much fun as we could.

Then it was Krissy, Dena and me. Then Dena and me.

Now, it was just me.

The lone wolf...

"You morose bitch," I muttered. Throwing my pen down, I leaned back and rubbed at my temples. "Stop feeling sorry for yourself."

It wasn't like I wasn't *happy* for my friends. Sure, I'd expected some of them – okay, I'd always expected Carrie to settle down. Find a nice guy, fall in love, and get married. She was that sort of girl. The one we'd always had to drag out, push toward the hot guy.

But then Krissy had gone and fallen in love too.

Then, it happened to Dena.

I was the last girl standing.

I'd always thought Krissy and I would be partying and living the life for...well...

Making a face, I snatched my pen. "You thought you'd be on the prowl with your BFF right up until you were fifty or something." A mental picture settled in my mind, the two of us still running around like we'd always done, hooking up with men half my age. I hoped I aged as well in reality as I did in my daydreams.

The image shifted to just me, and I found myself wondering just what I'd be doing in five years, ten years. All my friends had fallen in love. They were getting married, talking about babies. Even Dena had a live-in boyfriend. In a couple of years, they might all be sitting around on playdates with their kids, and I'd be going out clubbing alone.

A year ago, I would have laughed at the idea, but now, it just left me feeling kind of down.

Sighing, I looked back at the paperwork in front of me.

Sadly, it hadn't diminished at all during my bout of self-pity, and that pile still stood between me and the door.

The bad part of being self-employed...there was nobody left to pick up the slack for a vacation or illness.

I needed to get my ass in gear too.

I had less than an hour to make serious headway if I didn't want to be late.

It was the first time we'd actually had a chance to go out in *forever* and I wasn't going to miss it.

DENA'S BOYFRIEND WAS HOT.

Not pretty boy hot, just plain hot.

He also looked at her like she'd hung the moon.

They sat across from me, and when he wasn't talking to me, he was looking at her. There was a hint of possession, a hint of satisfaction, all mixed with a decidedly pleased smile.

It was like he was telling the world, *She's mine, everybody. Mine.*

Not bragging, really, just happy with it.

And that made him that much hotter.

There was something decidedly sexy about a man in love. Especially a man in love who didn't ignore everyone else.

When he looked over at me and asked how my practice was going, he seemed genuinely interested and talked about some of the cases – sans names, of course – some friends of his had worked back in Chicago. We made small talk, and Dena chatted about the move, and I wondered why in the hell I was feeling so down about the fact that my best friends were all happy.

"Man, service is so *slow* tonight," I said, looking longingly toward the kitchen. I wasn't one of those women who worried about her figure. When I was hungry, I ate...unless I forgot. "I never got around to eating lunch."

"Me, either." Dena made a face. "I'm getting the crash course from hell now. The new DA is really putting me through my paces."

"I bet you love it after that mess you had with the last boss."

She grinned. "Damned straight. This lawyer actually seems to care...you know...about being a lawyer."

"So he's not a total shark?" I said it lightly.

Dena stuck out her tongue. It was an ongoing joke between us. I hadn't gone into law for the same reasons my friends had. I had a good brain, I liked money, and I didn't like blood. When the time had come to start figuring out a career, a counselor in high school had said, *you know, you're smart enough. You could be a doctor or lawyer.*

Again, I didn't like blood.

I went with lawyer.

I liked helping people well enough, but that wasn't why I did it. For the most part, it didn't suck, and sometimes I even liked my job, but I doubted I found the satisfaction from it that Dena did. Maybe I was a shark, but I was a good lawyer, and my clients were typically satisfied with the job I did for them. Besides, I'd seen what happened when some people *didn't* have a shark, and it wasn't pretty.

"We live in a world full of barracudas, babe. Sometimes we need sharks." Arik lifted Dena's hand to his lips and kissed her knuckles. He must have been doing something else under the table, because Dena's lids fluttered a bit, and I saw her breathing catch.

A moment later, she cleared her throat and smiled at me. "Yeah. Besides, sometimes sharks make good friends."

"Spare me the kissing up." I made a face at her, but was spared the chore of trying to find something else to talk about – the weather was up next – when the server appeared with our food.

I didn't know when it became so hard to talk to my best friend, but for some reason, the things we normally talked about, now just didn't seem to fit.

And there was no way in *hell* I was going to tell her that I was suddenly feeling the pangs of losing her and the others. Not while Arik was there, nuzzling on her knuckles and toying with her thigh – or other body parts – under the table.

I wouldn't do that to her.

"YOU'VE BEEN QUIET TONIGHT."

Looking over at Dena as we walked down the sidewalk, I managed a strained smile. It had been good seeing her, nice getting to know Arik a little better, but...yeah, I'd been quiet. "I'm just tired." Managing a shrug, I added, "It's crazy at the office. I need to hire somebody to help out so I don't get behind the next time I need to go out of town, but in the meantime, I'm dealing with all the stuff that piled up while I was gone. My admin is great for paperwork and phones, but she's never worked with anybody in the legal area before, so I'd rather her not deal with anything important until I have time to teach her more."

Dena seemed to accept that.

"Krissy looked...well, she looked good, didn't she?" Dena asked after a few moments.

"Yeah." I felt a tug in my chest as I thought about the baby she lost. "She looked good. DeVon is taking care of her."

"I think they're both taking care of each other," Dena said. "He was pretty broken up too."

"Yeah." Blowing out a breath, I lifted my face to the sky. "I can't imagine what they went through."

"I don't want to."

We reached the end of the block and stopped. Dena was heading in one direction with Arik, me in another.

I wasn't just talking about heading home, either.

Feel sorry for yourself later, I reminded myself.

"Pizza in a couple of weeks?" Dena asked.

"Absolutely." I pressed a quick kiss to her cheek and nodded at Arik.

After hugging Dena, we went our separate ways, and I found myself wondering if the night out had been a good idea after all.

I'd wanted to see my friend, yet somehow, I now felt more alone than before.

TWO

LESLIE

The entire apartment smelled lemony clean and the surfaces of the appliances in my miniscule kitchen sparkled.

I, however, was sweaty and dusty.

After shoving the cleaning supplies into the small space at the top of my closet, I retreated to my bathroom – the shower stall sparkled too. I would have given my right arm for a long, hot soak, but my budget hadn't quite extended to where I could shell out the kind of cash it would take to afford an apartment that came with a tub.

At least not the kind of apartment I'd *want*.

If I'd stayed with Webster and Steinberg, I would have been able to upgrade already, but branching out on my own had taken a lot of cash. I was now seeing a slow, steady climb in my income, but it had taken cutting back on a lot of things and focusing on things that mattered.

Sadly, finding an apartment that came with a bathtub wasn't one of the things that mattered.

But it was in the plan.

In another year or so, I thought I'd be able to get a bigger place – and not just a *little* bigger.

I was waiting until I was secure enough to find *the* place.

I was nothing if not an excellent planner. And I had no problem with waiting to get what I really wanted.

Hot water from the shower pulsed down on tight shoulders, and I sighed, relaxing a little as sweat, dust and stress washed away down the drain. In a short while, I was going to be sweaty again and hopefully, I'd get rid of a lot *more* stress.

I was heading to the club and the plan was to find a man and spend the night under him, over him, in front of him. I needed sex and I needed to forget about all the brooding I'd been doing.

My life was *good*.

I was beautiful, successful and I was doing exactly what I'd planned to be doing just a few short years ago.

That my friends had chosen other paths didn't really matter. I had my *own* path and I was happy with it.

Yet, as I climbed out of the shower a few minutes later and dried off, a small voice in the back of my head seemed to whisper...*if you were happy, you wouldn't have to work so hard to make yourself believe it.*

CLUB PRIVÉ WAS a study in elegant debauchery.

Sitting at the bar on the VIP level, I sipped my drink and waved at Carrie once she saw me.

I was surprised she could.

Her eyes seemed locked and focused on Gavin, as if nothing else existed.

They'd just gotten back from their honeymoon and one might think they'd be okay to go a few seconds without staring at the other, but I guess that was what love did to you.

I wouldn't know. I just didn't understand love.

I'd had a few boyfriends I'd *liked*, that I'd cared about, but love?

No.

Carrie grinned at me as she dropped down on the bar stool next to me. "Look what the cat dragged in," she said, leaning over to hug me.

"I'm pretty sure cats can't drag in this." Smugly, I glanced down at myself, pleased with the vivid green of my barely-there dress. I stood out among all the black and the red, which had been the whole point.

My life motto, ironically, came from Dr. Seuss. *Why fit in when you were born to stand out?*

Carrie rolled her eyes at me. "One day, you just might find a guy with an ego to match yours."

"Why would I want to?" Shrugging, I sipped my drink and studied the men on the VIP level.

Carrie's husband, Gavin, owned the club – well, technically, they both did, I supposed. That was the only reason I had access to the VIP level. I couldn't afford it on my own – at least not yet. Although even once my own finances allowed it, I didn't plan on telling them I'd be happy to pay for it. If they were happy to give the membership to me, then I was happy to accommodate them. I wasn't cheap, per se. I just enjoyed nice things, and when I had somebody nice enough to provide me with such things free of charge, then who was I to argue?

Nobody on the VIP level was catching my eye, though. At least nobody who wasn't already paired up with somebody.

There was a sexy brunet at one table, who kept eying me, but he was with a woman, and while I might be shallow as hell, I didn't think much of a man who made eyes at me when he was clearly with somebody else.

Loyalty was one thing I *did* value.

In my opinion, it was something that was becoming more and more rare in the world. Even more so in my line of work.

"How has life been treating you?" Carrie asked.

"Busy." Grimacing, I shifted my attention back to her. "I'm going to have to hire somebody to help in the office, and the way business is picking up, I might need to hire a partner before too long."

"That's fantastic! You should be on cloud nine." She flagged down a server and asked for a drink before turning back to me. Her eyes narrowed shrewdly as she asked, "So why aren't you?"

Since when had I become that transparent?

I didn't know, but I wasn't about to explain my sullen mood over the past few days. Carrie would either see too much into it, or just not get it. Then again, *I* didn't get it.

She was right. I should be on cloud nine. My practice was doing fantastic, especially considering I'd barely been at it for a year. I'd splurged on a beautiful Michael Kors tote a few days ago and last month, a new pair of Jimmy Choos. I was even on target to take a trip to Europe next summer and was in the planning stages of it. It wouldn't be too long before I could move to a bigger, nice apartment. I was right on track with my plan. I had everything I thought I wanted.

And yet...

I pasted a smile on my face as Gavin suddenly appeared at our sides.

"My beautiful wife," he said, bending to kiss Carrie.

She leaned against him for a moment, and I busied myself with my nearly empty drink. Then it was a completely empty drink, and I got busy flagging down the server to order another one. By the time I'd done that, they'd surfaced from a deep, intimate kiss. It wasn't that public displays of affection bothered me – if they did, then Club Privé was the last place I should be.

But there was something between people like Carrie and Gavin, Krissy and DeVon – and now Dena and Arik – that was too intimate to simply sit and watch. That deep sort of connection was more than just affection, and it made me uncomfortable to witness. Some things were *too* private.

"Leslie, you're looking lovely tonight."

I swung my head around and smiled at Gavin, careful not to let anything I was thinking or feeling show on my face. Carrie had seen something. I could still see it in her eyes, but even if some part of me might have wanted to share with her, I wasn't about to do it with Gavin here.

Besides, what was I going to say?

It just dawned on me that I'm feeling kinda...

I didn't let myself finish that thought. If I didn't finish it, then I didn't have to deal with it.

Sometimes, the only way to deal with things was to *not* deal with things.

"And you're looking very..." I paused as I slid my eyes between him and Carrie. "Married."

He chuckled as he slid his arm around her waist. "I'll take that as a compliment."

"Do that," I said sincerely. And I did mean it that way. They looked wonderful together.

The server appeared at my side with my drink, and I accepted with a smile before looking toward the railing. Restlessness burned inside me, but I couldn't just up and walk away.

I was saved from further questions, though, when one of the men from the club's security team appeared at Gavin's side and bent his head to murmur in Gavin's ear. Gavin nodded and touched Carrie's arm. "We're needed."

Carrie gave me an apologetic smile and I waved her off. "Go. I want to dance anyway."

"I'll try to find you later."

"Please don't." I wagged my brows. "I'm hoping to be busy."

She laughed as Gavin took her hand. A moment later, they were gone, and I took my drink over to the railing. From the corner of my eye, I could see the man who'd been eying me finish his drink as the woman across the table from him abruptly stood up and stormed off.

The skin between my shoulder blades crawled, letting me know he was still watching me. Shit. I really didn't want to deal with some creep tonight. I kept my gaze locked on the dancers below me. Tossing back my drink, I pushed back from the railing and saw the creep dropping a few bills on the table. He slid a look my way, followed by a slow smile. I ignored him as I gave my empty glass to the server and headed for the stairs.

Time to exit stage left.

He caught up with me just a few feet from the stairs. I couldn't say I was surprised. Irritated, yes. But not surprised. I knew his type.

"Are you heading out already? He gave me a quick, charming smile. "I was just coming to ask if I could buy you a drink."

"I'm not thirsty." Keeping my voice cool, I cut around him. He wasn't so easily dissuaded, though.

I had one foot on the steps leading down to the lower level when he joined me.

"A dance, then, perhaps?"

Instead of answering right away, I continued my way down the stairs, and on the landing between the levels, I moved over to the railing and tipped my head back to look up at him. His precisely styled hair didn't move at all as he dipped his head to meet my eyes.

"No dance," I said levelly. "No drink. You're not my type."

His lids flickered a bit at that and a muscle tightened in his jaw. He hadn't liked that. He recovered quickly, though, flashing me a smile that was without a doubt one of the best I'd ever seen.

It did absolutely nothing for me.

"Oh, come on...I bet I can prove you wrong. A drink..." He traced a fingertip down my cheek. "A dance. I bet we could have a lot of...fun."

Deliberately I stepped away from him, working to control my temper. While I didn't believe in stereotyping, my own red curls and hot-headedness didn't go far to dispelling *that* particular myth.

I made my voice icy. "Somehow, I really doubt that."

I pushed past him, and this time, when he tried to follow, I nodded to the security guard at the foot of the stairs. "If you don't step back now, I'm going to tell that guy down there you're putting your hands on me without permission. Don't be surprised if your VIP membership goes on instant probation."

His face screwed up. "You lying bitch."

"You touched my face." Giving him a cat's smile, I shrugged. "I didn't invite your touch or give you permission. In fact, I'd told you *no*. I'm pretty sure that the rules clearly say when told *no*, you're supposed to accept and move on."

Sure, I was being extremely literal with the rules, but the guy was a sleaze. Chances were there were more than a few women here he'd already gotten too hands-on with. This time, he'd picked the wrong one. I didn't *get* pushed around – I might push, and push hard, but nobody tried it with me.

His jaw clenched and his face flushed, but he didn't say anything else, just cut around me, keeping a wide distance. He hesitated at the top of the steps and it didn't take long to see why. The big guy clad in the discreet suit Gavin preferred his security team to wear was staring dead at him. The look wasn't happy.

By the time I cleared the steps, the two of them were having a quiet conversation that he didn't appear to be enjoying.

I didn't spare him another look as I lost myself on the dance floor.

AN HOUR LATER, I was finishing up a bottle of water when somebody bumped into me – and hard.

I crashed into the person next to me, felt my ankle giving out.

Already prepared to fall, I wind milled my arms anyway.

I didn't fall though.

Strong forearms came around my waist and a heated body pressed against mine.

My heart skipped a beat in appreciation.

The scent of clean male sweat filled my head, and I looked up, not quite ready to get hopeful. But then I met his eyes and hope started to race alongside my pulse.

Dark brown eyes held mine.

"I...I'm sorry." Feeling a little breathless, I smiled up at him. "Excuse me."

"Please don't." He smiled and when he did, his teeth flashed white against the short, neat growth of his beard.

I had dirty images of just how that beard might feel against my girl parts and his response took a minute to process. "Um... what? Please don't what?"

"Excuse yourself. As a matter of fact, feel free to fall into my arms anytime you want." He helped steady me, but didn't let go of my arms right away and I didn't mind a bit. As a matter of fact, he could have held on a little longer.

"Well, aren't you a flirt."

"Not much of a flirt. I just speak my mind. And if you

hadn't fallen against me, I wouldn't have gotten a hold of you." He held out a hand, that wicked, sexy smile still on his lips. "Maybe you'll dance with me and let me hold you again?"

I put my hand in his. "Maybe I'll do just that."

THREE
PAXTON

"We didn't do too bad."

Looking up, I met the eyes of Decker Marley, the man who'd played lead guitar for me ever since I'd first started singing. He was also my best friend, and I knew by the look in his eyes that he was being...polite.

"Hey, fuck that. I think we nailed it." Joker Trammel spun his drumsticks around, grinning at us as he jogged down the steps to join us at the door. "We fucking kicked *ass*. We ought to tell.

Brinke to get sick more often."

Get sick was delivered with a roll of his eyes.

The rest of the band laughed, save for Decker and me. Brinke was our main backup singer – and my wife. She told me she'd meet me at the studio this morning. She never had.

My texts had gone unanswered as well.

We needed to talk once I got back to the penthouse because this bullshit wasn't going to keep happening.

"So, are we going to recut the songs we did today?" Decker asked, ignoring the rest of the crew.

"No." Staring outside the double doors into the busy New

York streets, I blew out a breath and then turned to look at everybody. They all looked more than a little surprised, but thankfully, none of them seemed upset. In fact, they looked relieved. "No. Brinke knows we're on a deadline. She'll understand."

"The fans might not." Joker was the one to voice what all of us were thinking.

Rubbing the back of my neck, I nodded. "Yeah. We'll cross that bridge when we come to it. But we can't keep holding up work on the new album because of..."

I couldn't even say the lie this time.

Brinke wasn't sick – not physically at least – and I had a bad feeling I knew why she wasn't there. She'd been out late last night, partying like we were still nineteen, without a care or responsibility. She didn't get that our lives couldn't go on like that anymore.

"Brinke." Decker said it for me. Moving up, he clapped a big hand on my shoulder. "Dude, look, you love her. We get that. But this shit – it ain't good for you. Ain't good for the band. Ain't good for your career – or ours."

He didn't even mention Brinke's career, because, without me to keep her going, she probably wouldn't have one. And I didn't say the other thing, that I wasn't even sure I did love her. Not like this.

The energy we'd had going today – *without* Brinke – I missed that. Just being able to lose myself in the music again, without being caught up in her drama had been amazing. But she was my wife – and more.

I sighed. "I gotta go. You all heading out?"

"Nah." He shrugged and looked back at everybody else. "I think we're going to head out, hit a club maybe. Guess you're not up for it."

"Not today."

I hitched my gig bag over my shoulder, then pulled out a ball cap and a pair of sunglasses. The others were doing the same. It was surprisingly easy to stay somewhat anonymous in the city with just a little effort.

"Okay, man." He punched me lightly on the shoulder. "Take it easy, Pax."

A few minutes later, I was tucked up in the back of a cab with my eyes closed.

Some of the guys wondered how I could do that, relax in the back of a New York City taxi. But I'd ridden in cabs in Beijing, New Delhi, and Mexico City – so had they. I figured if I'd survived those, then a driver from the Big Apple was a cakewalk.

I came awake to the sound of a heavy fist pounding on the glass between the driver and me. Groggily, I blinked my eyes a few times, then looked over and saw the towering spire that housed my penthouse. It wasn't exactly what I'd planned for a home here, but Brinke had fallen in love with it, and sometimes it was just easier to give in to her when it wasn't something important.

I'd gone along with it, and now I had to admit, the place was a lot more convenient than a house a little bit out of the city. Not to mention what a bitch it would've been to drive back and forth on the days we needed to be in the studio. Still, I wanted a *house*. Someplace with a yard and grass. Maybe we'd do that later. We could always keep the penthouse, stay here when we were recording, use it for guests and that sort of thing.

I pushed money into the slot to pay the fare, along with the tip, and mumbled thanks, still half-asleep.

By the time I hit the elevator bank, though, I was awake. Awake and hungry. We'd ordered in Chinese for lunch, and that had stuck with me for maybe an hour. I wanted a steak – one the size of Kansas. Maybe we could all –

The second I stepped out of the elevator, I knew I wouldn't be inviting Brinke out anywhere. Hell, she'd be lucky if I didn't *kick* her ass out.

Music blasted from the system we'd just installed last week.

Next to my right foot, a puddle of what looked like vomit spread across the polished hardwood floors that Brinke had cooed over. A bottle of wine was spilled on the antique Aubusson rug she'd insisted we *had* to have, and there was a box of half-eaten pizza on the couch *I* had wanted. The stains from tomato sauce looked like they were already smeared in.

Over the souring smell of vomit mingled with wine, I caught the familiar odor of marijuana and booze, food and cigarettes. The cigarette smoke was so thick it hung in a thick haze around the apartment, and I felt my jaw locking on me. There was a couple on the fat armchair I'd put by the windows so I could look outside at night, and I slammed my fist against the lights as I realized the two of them were screwing right there in my living room.

Two sets of glassy eyes turned toward me. The woman smiled, then giggled. "Heya, Pax...wanna join us?"

"Get out."

I recognized her vaguely. She was one of the girls Brinke liked to party with. "Get out," I said again. "And don't bother coming back. I'm telling building security you're not allowed in anymore."

While she continued to blink at me, confused, I grabbed the phone and waited for the front desk to pick up – another thing to like about the building.

I relayed my message while the couple by the window started to move again, low moans reaching my ears – and the guy on the phone. "Ah...Mr. Gorham, do you require assistance?"

"I think I require a lot – but not the kind you can give me.

Just remember what I said, and make sure *everybody* knows." Then I slammed the phone down and strode to the chair.

Drawing back my foot, I kicked it hard enough that it skidded, even with the two of them screwing on it like wild rabbits.

When they looked at me this time, there was sense in their eyes. At least a little. "You've got two minutes to be out of here, or you'll be arrested for trespassing."

Every single person up here would be stopped on the way out, and none of them would be coming back. Brinke's friend – Sanja? Sanya? I couldn't remember – gaped at me, but her partner got it. He stood up, and she would've fallen if he hadn't caught her.

"Come on, Pax," she said, her voice slurred. "Why so mad?"

"Get out."

"Come on, Jay," he said, finally managing to zip his jeans. He had the decency to smooth her skirt down, never once lifting his head to acknowledge me.

It was Sanja then.

From the corner of my eyes, I saw somebody looking at me from the kitchen. I pointed at her – no, them. Another couple came slinking around. "Get out."

Before moving away from the door, I pulled my phone out and pulled up the number for building security and called down, giving terse instructions to watch for the people leaving my penthouse. "First of them coming down now – remember, they are *never* allowed back in my place again. *Ever.*"

"Hey..." Sanja said, a whine entering her voice. "You can't do that. Brinke and I are best friends. I come see her all the time."

"Yeah. When you want to get high and don't have any money." Curling my lip at her, I stepped aside and pointed to the door. "I'm the one who paid for the place. It's my name on all the papers. Now get out."

Brinke couldn't be trusted to sign for anything as important as our home. She'd given a two-hundred-thousand dollar car to cover some debts to a dealer a couple years back. I'd told her then that my name was going on everything, and that if I caught her trying to give away or sell any of it, I'd send her to jail for theft.

She'd cried, yelled, smacked me and thrown things.

I hadn't given in that time, and I'd never regretted it.

My stomach twisted as the door slammed shut behind the people I'd just kicked out. That better be the last...

Disgusted, I stopped in front of the guest bedroom and opened the door to find a mini-orgy going on. Four people took up the massive custom king bed. I hit the light and held up my phone. "You've got five minutes to get out or I call the cops."

Like Sanja and the others, they were so strung out, it took a few seconds for my words to penetrate. When it did, one tried to argue, but I cut her off. "Brinke doesn't own this place. I do. Get out or I'll have you arrested. *Now!*"

I didn't bother to see if they listened. I'd called the cops if they weren't gone. I had no problem with that.

I strode to the end of the hall and looked toward our bedroom. I saw Brinke lying on the floor of the guest bathroom just ahead of me, but I ignored her. She wasn't who I cared–

"Ah, hell, no..." The door to Carter's room was open. I took off at a run.

I burst inside, already processing the low moans. Hitting the lights, I stared at the couple on my little girl's canopy style bed. It was round and outfitted with sheer drape-like scarves that hung from the top. She'd seen it and the look on her face had sealed the deal without her asking. She'd wanted a princess bed, and my little girl had gotten her damn princess bed.

"Get out!" I didn't even remember crossing the room or grabbing the man.

He was just on the floor, staring at me. The woman screamed and I half-turned toward her.

"Where is my daughter?"

They gaped at me, confused.

"Dude...she..."

The guy rubbed at his face, and then reached down, scratched at the curls near his still swollen dick. Fury exploded through me. I grabbed him off the floor and hauled him out into the hall, slamming him against the wall. "Where is my daughter?"

"She went into the closet, dude! We told her we needed the bed...she seemed cool with it!" He blinked at me, looking confused.

A second later, he looked unconscious – and bloody – because I'd all but punched his teeth through the other side of his head.

They'd put my little girl in the closet so they could fuck in her bed.

I was going to...

Breathe...

I forced myself to do just that as I turned and looked at the woman. She was still screaming and sobbing, her hands scrabbling at Carter's pink and purple bedspread. She didn't matter. He didn't matter. Only my baby girl did.

"Get out of that bedroom now unless you want to be arrested," I said, barely able to squeeze the words out through my fury. "Get. Out. Now."

She half fell off the bed and started to reach for the blanket to cover herself.

"Touch that and spend the night in jail."

Her hand fell away and she crawled toward her clothes. Ignoring her, I moved toward the closet.

It was closed, but under it, I saw a thin beam of light. Carter kept flashlights everywhere. She was afraid of the dark. Maybe a lot of kids her age were.

What in the hell had they said to make her go into the closet?

I started to grab the handle but stopped at the sight of blood on my knuckles.

Swearing, I shrugged out of the black button-down I'd worn over my t-shirt and used it to clean the blood from my hand. It wasn't perfect, but I wasn't leaving my daughter in there a minute longer.

She was crouched there, sitting with her back against the wall, and the little camping styled lamp by her feet. It was decorated with Disney princesses, and she held a bow and arrow – Princess Merida, of course – tightly.

She peeked up at me. "There's monsters, Daddy."

My heart broke a little. "No, baby," I said, shaking my head.

"There's monsters. I was having nightmares, and then they came in, and I screamed, and they said I had to be quiet and hide or the monsters would get me. Is it zombies?" Carter's big eyes stared up at me and I wanted to punch something – or someone. Again.

Brinke let Carter watch zombie shows a couple weeks ago, and now, instead of whatever kind of monsters kids *should* dream of, Carter thought zombies were real and might come get her.

"I told you, sweetheart. Those zombies are just make-up and pretend. They aren't real. Come on. Whatever monsters were here? I got rid of them."

CARTER LAY SLEEPING on the big, beautiful bed of the Waldorf Astoria's presidential suite.

Brinke had been passed out when I finally checked on her, so deep under that I'd ended up letting hotel security contact a doctor – *he's discreet, I assure you.*

I hoped like hell whoever they'd called was discreet, but that wasn't my main concern.

Carter was.

And because I had to think about my baby, I'd been sitting in the chair by the window, staring outside for the past hour as I came to the understanding that I had to do something. I couldn't just push it aside anymore.

The woman I'd fallen in love with was pretty much gone.

And the guy I'd been then? He didn't even exist anymore.

When we found out she was pregnant –

Shit. No big mystery there. I'd grown up. Remembering the shit my parents had put me through, some of the stories that Brinke had told me about her folks, I'd known. The moment we'd looked at that little plus sign and realized we were going to have a baby, I'd known that things had to change.

Brinke had seemed to get it too. But either she hadn't meant it or she'd forgotten.

And I didn't care anymore.

Whatever we once had was over.

We were done.

Carter made a low noise under her breath, something that sounded almost like a little puppy whimpering.

Getting up, I went over to the big bed and settled down in the middle, pulling her in close to me. She snuggled up to me and the crying stopped immediately.

"It's okay, princess," I said softly. "Nobody's going to hurt you. You're safe."

I'd make sure of it too.

No matter what.

FOUR

LESLIE

I came awake in a bed that wasn't mine, tucked up next to a hard, warm male body, and I put together pieces of a puzzle I wasn't aware existed until I'd already solved it.

I wasn't at home.

I hadn't spent the night alone.

Also, it was a little later in the morning than I liked. I only realized that when I saw the glowing red numbers on the clock on the table next to my head.

It was almost ten.

I needed to get home.

When I stirred, the man next to me grunted and rolled onto his belly, but he didn't wake.

After a moment, I eased onto my side and stared at him, waiting for my mind to clear.

Bit by bit, it did.

The guy – we'd met at Club Privé. He'd stopped me from falling. We'd danced. Had a few drinks.

Then we ended up here.

A few random flashes pierced the haze of alcohol and good,

hard sex. I ached in a nice way, but beyond that, I couldn't say much about the past night. Not the first time that'd happened.

Easing out of the bed, I looked around for my clothes and gathered them up.

My head pounded a little, and I grabbed my purse as well, hoping I'd remembered to throw some sort of over the counter pain killer in there.

If not, I could always drown myself under the shower.

TWENTY MINUTES LATER, I was showered, and after having dry-swallowed two ibuprofen tablets, I felt something closer to normal. My dress from last night was wrinkled, but it would do for now. My panties would not – they'd been ripped. I tossed them into the garbage, relieved to see numerous condom wrappers in there. That was always the risk when mixing alcohol and sex.

Spying my shoes by the bed, I bent to pick them up.

"Hey, beautiful."

Shoes in hand, I looked back over my shoulder to see my partner from last night pushing up on his elbow. The hotel we'd chosen to come was across the street from Club Privé. It was pristine, discreet, elegant, and nicer than some other places I'd woken up.

A thin strip of sunlight came through the mostly closed drapes to fall across his face, highlighting the bronzed beauty of his features. Dreads secured in a neat tail at his neck left that fantastic face unframed, and I knew I'd enjoyed the view of that face from multiple angles most of the night.

But I needed to go.

He trailed a finger down my spine.

I looked away.

Dammit.

"When can I see you again?"

I'd done this often enough that I'd perfected my exit strategy. It helped that I never left the club with a creep. The security guys and I had developed our own little silent language. If I was with some guy who managed to slide under my radar, but who they knew was going to be a problem, they let me know. I'd only needed their intervention twice, though. I'd developed a pretty decent radar when it came to creeps.

This guy wasn't one.

He was, however, someone I needed to let down easy.

Swiveling around, I crawled across the bed and knelt over him.

Giving him a quick kiss, I pulled back and smiled down at him.

"Last night was fun...but that's all it was. I'm not looking for anything else."

He grimaced at me. "Ouch." One hand slid higher on my thigh. "Sure I can't change your mind?"

I brushed my mouth across his. "Yes. But thanks for the offer."

He hauled me down for one more kiss and I had to admit, my heart was fluttering harder when he let go, but by the time I was on the street less than ten minutes later, I couldn't even quite remember the exact color of his eyes.

And I knew by the time I was home, I'd forgotten a lot more about my one-night stand.

It was sad, really, but it proved what I'd already known. Love wasn't for me.

———

THE RÉSUMÉS on the left were going in the shredder as soon

as I got up to refill my wine. The ones on the right, I'd go through again. I had a good feeling about two of them, and the others were decent possibilities.

One thing was certain – I was hiring somebody within the next few weeks, before I drowned in paperwork.

I could see my own obituary.

Leslie Calvin – she died buried under mounds of paperwork. Those who knew her best believe she would be pissed off – she always wanted to die dancing.

Leaving the firm that had given me my first job hadn't been a bad idea, but I hadn't been prepared for how much work came with going solo. The paperwork alone was enough to make me want to pull my hair out.

And not everything was even connected to cases.

Like advertising.

That was next on my list of things to conquer for the day, and it was my least favorite.

With a headache pounding at the base of my skull, I flipped to the final résumé in my pile. Within a split second, I wadded it up and hurled it across the room.

"No, I don't think somebody with two years working as a filing clerk will count as experience," I muttered. "Paralegal experience a *necessity*. Not optional. A *necessity*. Maybe I should've mentioned a basic understanding of the English language."

Leaning back in my chair, I stared up at the tray-ceiling overhead.

The ceiling fan spun in slow, lazy circles. Outside my windows, I heard the hum of the city. I wanted to get out there in that hum, leaving the monotony of work for another day and just *do* something. That restlessness that had plagued me for days – weeks – longer – wasn't letting up, but I couldn't think of anything that might relieve it.

Nor could I understand why I was feeling it.

I had a great job.

I had a decent social life.

A year ago, I would have been completely happy to sit here and work my afternoon away. Work hard, play harder. Earn money, spend money.

What had changed? Had *I* changed?

I had a funny feeling the answer was yes. And I had an even funnier feeling that I knew when that change had started.

But I didn't want to think about any of that too much, didn't want to put a finger on it.

Naming it would just make it worse anyway.

End of preview.
Club Prive continues in *A Legal Affair (Club Prive Book 9)*, available now.

ABOUT THE AUTHOR

M. S. Parker is a USA Today Bestselling author and the author of the Erotic Romance series, Club Privè and Chasing Perfection.

Living in Las Vegas, she enjoys sitting by the pool with her laptop writing on her next spicy romance.

Growing up all she wanted to be was a dancer, actor or author. So far only the latter has come true but M. S. Parker hasn't retired her dancing shoes just yet. She is still waiting for the call for her to appear on Dancing With The Stars.

When M. S. isn't writing, she can usually be found reading–oops, scratch that! She is always writing.

For more information:
www.msparker.com
msparkerbooks@gmail.com

 facebook.com/msparkerauthor

ACKNOWLEDGMENTS

First, I would like to thank all of my readers. Without you, my books would not exist. I truly appreciate each and every one of you.

A big "thanks" goes out to all the Facebook fans, street team, beta readers, and advanced reviewers. You are a HUGE part of the success of all my series.

I have to thank my PA, Shannon Hunt. Without you my life would be a complete and utter mess. Also a big thank you goes out to my editor Lynette and my wonderful cover designer, Sinisa. You make my ideas and writing look so good.